BEYOND THE RED BELLY

MARGOT BOSONNET

ILLUSTRATED BY SARAH CUNNINGHAM

WOLFHOUND PRESS
Celebrating 25 *Years*

First published in 1999 by
Wolfhound Press Ltd
68 Mountjoy Square
Dublin 1, Ireland
Tel: (353-1) 874 0354
Fax: (353-1) 872 0207

The Arts Council
An Chomhairle Ealaíon

Wolfhound Press receives financial assistance from the Arts Council/An Chomhairle Ealaíon, Dublin, Ireland.

British Library Cataloguing in Publication Data
A catalogue record for this book is available from the British Library.

ISBN 0-86327-755-1

10 9 8 7 6 5 4 3 2 1

Cover Illustration: Sarah Cunningham
Typesetting: Wolfhound Press
Printed in the UK by Cox & Wyman Ltd, Reading, Berks.

Contents

1	Here We Go Again	7
2	Harold Sets a Challenge	11
3	Up the Red Belly	19
4	Races and Riots	25
5	Interesting Business	34
6	A Big Shock	42
7	A Sad Farewell	50
8	Disaster Strikes	56
9	The Police Take an Interest	66
10	Preparations	71
11	The Protest March	77
12	Into Action	83
13	The Long Sit	94
14	In the Dark of Night	107
15	Another Day	119
16	Revenge	128
17	Felicity Makes a Decision	133
18	New Developments	142
19	Red Belly	150
20	Unexpected Happenings	159
21	Facing Things	166
22	Aftermath	172
23	A New Beginning	179
24	Trouble	187
25	Reach for the Sky	197

'Columbus! ...

   'Columbus! ...

   'Christopher Co-luum-bus!'

Mackey battled his way to the very bottom of the woods — away from the Red Belly, away from the Captain's Table, away from the Tunnel. Every few feet he stopped to call and listen. Overhead, the tangle of trees met in a dense canopy, letting in only the odd stray beam of light. It was dark and dank and sinisterly threatening.

The hollow log lay in a bed of moss, frail, leggy toadstools growing from its crevices. There were little treasures hidden deep in the log — bits and pieces of things. Mackey sometimes came here to search its crumbling insides. But he wasn't after little treasures today. He was after Columbus.

Down at this end of the woods, the ditch was wide and deep and filled with stagnant water. Brambles lined the banks — though wild raspberries grew there too, tempting, juicy scarlet jewels. This was the home of the rats — big, fierce rats that guarded their territory well and often sent the gang running for their lives.

Mackey called again. *'Columbus!'*

There was a scuffle and a tearing of bushes ahead, then a loud splash. Mackey ran.

The dark water churned below the brambles, so that for a moment Mackey couldn't see what was there. Then Columbus emerged — slimy, dirty, dripping wet, with a dead rat between his jaws.

At least, Mackey hoped it was dead.

'Drop it, boy! Drop it!'

Columbus dived to one side, but Mackey put out a leg, blocking his way. Quick as lightning, Columbus shot around Mackey's other side and tore off up the woods with his booty, leaving Mackey standing there, exasperated.

'Pesky dog!' he muttered. He started up the woods after Columbus. He knew better than to run. Columbus could fly like the wind; there was no catching him. Mackey had learnt that lesson long ago. With the danger area now behind, it didn't matter so much any more.

When Mackey reached the Red Belly clearing, he was met by a hail of earth. Columbus had just finished digging a deep hole right beneath the Red Belly tree itself. He dropped his precious rat in, then reversed and, with his back legs working like pistons, sent the pile of earth splattering hard against the trunk of the tree. It fell back down, neatly filling up the hole. Columbus examined his handiwork critically, then cocked his leg and watered the whole thing.

Mackey grabbed him by the collar, almost knocking him off balance. 'Stupid dog!' he roared. He crouched down and waved a warning finger at Columbus. 'Wanta die of poisoning? I told you to stay away from rats!'

Columbus wagged his tail and licked Mackey full in the face.

'Yuck!' Mackey recoiled in disgust, remembering where that tongue had last been. He stood up. 'C'mon!' Dragging Columbus by the collar, he headed through the woods towards home.

When they reached the laneway behind the houses, Columbus started to struggle, and once they were through the gateway into Mackey's garden, he sat down. Mackey dragged him up the garden path. Columbus protested all the way, digging in his heels.

'Stoppit!' Mackey roared. 'Wanta choke yourself?'

It appeared that Columbus did, preferring that to the fate that awaited him.

They reached the garden tap. Mackey filled the bucket that he kept beneath it, then quickly dunked Columbus's face in the water.

'Wash out your mouth,' he ordered.

Columbus came up spluttering and looked at Mackey pathetically. Mackey dunked him again. Then again. Finally he picked up the bucket and emptied the water over Columbus. Columbus shook himself frantically, spraying Mackey and the surrounding area with mud.

There was a loud rapping overhead.

'Here we go again!' muttered Mackey, as the bedroom window opened and his mother's head emerged.

Mrs McCarthy was small and dark like Mackey, but very pretty. Felicity said she was the prettiest mother she'd ever seen. She could also be the fiercest, and the gang were somewhat wary of her.

She surveyed the muddy scene below, her face a mixture of disbelief and resignation.

'Ignatius McCarthy! It's only ten o'clock in the morning, and look at the pair of you!'

'Columbus was just exploring,' Mackey defended him quickly.

'Explore! I'll *explore* that dog!' Mrs McCarthy exploded. 'Lock him up in the shed until I've time to give him a proper bath, and get in here yourself for the same.'

She slammed the window shut.

'Now look what you've done!' scolded Mackey, taking hold of Columbus's collar again. He hauled Columbus over to the shed, opened the door and shoved him in. Columbus backed into a corner and sat down, water forming a pool around him.

'Pesky dog!' said Mackey softly, lovingly.

He went out and shut the door.

Later on, when all the fuss was over, Mackey and Columbus went looking for the gang.

They weren't up the Red Belly — the giant tree, with the splash of red paint on its trunk, that formed their headquarters — but Mackey found them further along the woods, sprawled over the Captain's Table.

The Captain's Table was a huge fallen tree on the edge of a clearing. Its roots spiralled into the air like the spokes of a wheel, and the branches were great fun for bouncing up and down on. This had been the gang's meeting-place before Felicity was able to climb the Red Belly. Now it was in dispute.

A big notice was pinned to one end of the trunk:

PRIVATE PROPERTY
KEEP OFF!
THIS TREE IS THE PROPERTY OF
THE YELLOW BELLY GANG.
TRESPASSERS WILL BE PERSECUTED.
SIGNED: HAROLD HANLEY (LEADER)

The Red Belly gang had been good enough to give part of their territory to Harold, a younger boy from across the road who wanted to form a gang of his own. They had told him he could have the trees around the clearing where the Captain's Table lay.

Harold had painted a yellow splodge on the trunk of one of the trees and called it the Yellow Belly. It was bad enough having him be a copycat like that; but, even worse, he'd assumed that the Captain's Table was

11

part of the deal. This had caused a lot of trouble last summer, and the matter was still unresolved.

'Why are you lot on the Captain's Table?' Mackey asked. 'Where's Harold?'

'There's been no sign of him all morning,' answered Jonathan. 'Anyway, it's really ours — why shouldn't we use it?'

'I'd nearly forgotten how nice it is here,' said Felicity. She was lying full-length on the Captain's Table, sunning herself. Felicity was Jonathan's twin, though she didn't look a bit like him. Jonathan was blond and tanned; Felicity had mousy hair and freckles.

Muggins was bouncing on one of the branches. Columbus started jumping up and down beside him, barking wildly.

'OK, Columbus,' Muggins laughed, 'I'll give you a go. Lift him up, Mackey.'

'He's too big to lift,' Mackey protested. 'He weighs a ton. Anyway, he's still all damp after his bath.'

'Why was he having a bath?' Felicity asked.

'He's been chasing rats again.'

'How utterly disgusting!' declared Joan, tossing her short dark hair. 'Mackey, you'll just have to keep him away from Kevin. I'm sorry, but that's it. He might give him some awful disease.'

'I've washed out his mouth,' said Mackey defensively, 'and my ma gave him a really good scrub.'

'Still and all ....' Joan was looking at Columbus doubtfully. 'We don't want to take any chances.'

Joan's little brother, Kevin, was fifteen months old and had just started walking. Mackey, to everyone's surprise, had taken a shine to him from the very beginning. Mackey himself was an only child, and his mum and dad were separated. When Joan had found out that he'd once had a sister who died, she'd appointed Mackey Kevin's big brother. Mackey took the position very seriously, which had landed him in a lot of trouble last year. He didn't want any more trouble now, so he quickly changed the subject.

'Orla not around?'

'She's up the village, chasing fellas,' sniggered Muggins, bouncing his branch really hard.

'She's weird these days, anyway,' Joan observed.

'And she hardly ever comes climbing any more,' Felicity complained. 'She's not even interested in the Red Belly.'

'I know,' Muggins said. 'She's driving my mum mad. She doesn't want to do anything around the house or mind the little ones any more. She keeps telling Mum to make me do it instead.' He pulled a face.

The gang were silent.

The change in Orla had been quite remarkable.

Orla was the eldest in her family; Muggins came next. As there were only ten months between them, Mrs Duggan had kept Orla back so that she and Muggins could start school together. But there were four younger ones too. Orla had always done more than her share of looking after them, and never, ever, complained.

Then, one day, she'd cut off all her beautiful curly red hair with nail scissors and gelled the bits that were left into spikes. She'd varnished her fingernails and toenails black, then announced that she couldn't do any more housework as it would chip her varnish. These days she spent her time patrolling the village like some mad-looking traffic warden. It was an astonishing about-turn that had left the rest of the gang feeling confused and somewhat taken aback. It was as if they were dealing with a stranger.

Columbus let out a loud snore, breaking the silence. He had fallen asleep in a patch of sunlight, finally exhausted after his morning's exertions.

'I see he's been digging under the Red Belly again,' Jonathan said.

Mackey grinned.

'If he digs any more holes there, the tree will fall down,' Joan declared dramatically.

'Don't be daft,' said Mackey. 'They're only little holes.'

'Yes, but they're all around the roots now,' Joan persisted. 'It's bound to have a bad effect. Anyway, it looks awful, and the ground gets so mucky when it rains. You should stop him, Mackey.'

'Want me to stop the rain, too?'

'It's not the same thing. You need to bring him to dog-training school, like Harold did with Arnie. Arnie always does as he's told.'

'Goody-goody!' muttered Mackey under his breath.

'Joan has a point,' said Jonathan.

'No she doesn't,' Mackey burst out indignantly. 'Send Columbus to school! Anybody here love school? No, I didn't think so. Why should I do that to poor Columbus? He's a free spirit, an explorer — he'd hate it .... Anyway, I'm training him myself.'

'I wish you'd hurry up and start,' grumbled Joan.

'I have started,' Mackey said defensively, 'only these things take time. He's still a puppy — he's not a year old yet.'

'Talking of school,' Felicity broke in, changing the subject before a real argument could break out, 'it's funny us not belonging anywhere now.'

'We do belong,' said Jonathan. 'We're enrolled in the secondary school in the village.'

'Yes, but that's not until September. We haven't actually gone there yet. But we've left our old school for good. It feels weird being sort of in-between.'

Jonathan laughed, but Muggins agreed. 'I know what you mean. I feel just the same.'

'So do I, a bit,' admitted Joan.

'We're like those stateless people who don't have any country to call their own,' Felicity went on. 'We don't have a school to call our own right now. We don't belong anywhere.'

'We belong to Conker Woods,' Muggins said.

'Yeah,' agreed Mackey. 'Three cheers for Conker Woods!'

'And the Red Belly,' Felicity added.

Mackey stuck a clenched fist into the air. 'Up the Red Belly!' he shouted. 'Up the Red Belly!'

The sound echoed around the woods, but Columbus merely sighed deeply and continued sleeping.

'What's all the racket about?'

The gang turned as Harold came into the clearing. He was on his own.

'Nothing,' said Mackey.

'You're making a lot of noise about nothing,' Harold observed.

'What's it to you?' Mackey challenged him.

'You're sitting on my territory.'

'So?'

Harold pointed at his notice.

'Oh, that thing!' Mackey was scathing. 'It belongs to last summer.'

'Nothing's changed,' Harold said firmly.

'We let you in on our sleep-out,' Mackey reminded him.

'He was in on it, all right,' giggled Muggins, remembering how Harold had scared the wits out of them all.

'You didn't have much choice,' Harold said. 'And that doesn't give you the right to grab what's mine, anyway.'

'It's not yours, it's ours,' Jonathan insisted. 'We never actually gave it to you.'

'Oh, no! We're not going to start all that again,' wailed Joan. 'Didn't we have enough of it last summer?'

There was a short silence. They were, indeed, fed up

with the subject of the Captain's Table — but what was to be done about it?

'As a matter of fact, I've been thinking ....' Harold said.

'With what?' Mackey jeered.

Harold ignored Mackey and went on, 'We can all use the Captain's Table, but somebody's got to own it officially, to have first rights.'

'That's fair enough,' agreed Jonathan.

'So ... I was thinking we could have a competition, to decide who owns it once and for all.'

'What sort of competition?'

'A race, from the very bottom of the woods to the very top — a race up in the trees only.'

'You mean like tree-chasing?' Felicity asked.

'That's it.' Harold nodded.

Tree-chasing was one of their favourite games. The woods contained lots of brilliant climbing trees; and there were half-fallen trees, too, that leaned against other trees, making ramps and jump-off points. In tree-chasing, you could go as high as you liked, or jump from tree to tree; but if you put a foot on the ground, you were out. So far they had mostly played it in the circle of trees around the Red Belly clearing, and, before that, around Harold's Yellow Belly clearing, but they'd never thought of doing Conker Woods from top to bottom. The idea appealed to them greatly.

'Is it possible?' asked Felicity, trying to think how the various trees fitted together.

'I figure it is,' said Harold. 'I've been looking. I don't see why not.'

'When?' asked Jonathan.

'Tomorrow. I don't have my gang here today. Billy and Mark had to stay at home.'

'That'll give us time to suss it out, too,' Mackey agreed.

Joan was frowning. 'I don't understand. How does it work, exactly?'

'What do you mean, how does it work?' Jonathan answered impatiently. 'We get up into the trees at the bottom of the woods and race all the way to the top.'

'But there's more of us than of them. Even if Orla won't do it, that's still five against three.'

'Ah ... I was coming to that,' said Harold.

Columbus chose that moment to wake up. He stretched himself, yawned, then tried to piddle against Harold's leg. Harold skipped out of the way fast and got up on the Captain's Table beside Felicity, who shoved over a bit to make room for him. He looked at Columbus with distaste. Mackey was watching Harold with narrowed eyes, ready to jump to Columbus's defence, but Harold said nothing.

'Go on,' said Joan. 'You were coming to what?'

'Well ....' Harold's face, behind his gold-rimmed glasses, became serious. He looked like a busy executive about to put a master plan before a board meeting. 'It's like this. We can't all be in the race anyway, because somebody's got to stay on the ground.'

'Why?' asked Muggins.

'To make sure nobody cheats.'

The others hadn't thought of that.

'Right,' Jonathan said, trying to take charge of things. 'So two people have to stay below, one from each gang. We'll draw lots.'

'No ... just hold on a minute.' Harold raised his hand. 'It's not as easy as that. We have to have even numbers, too.'

Jonathan eyed Harold impatiently. 'But if one of your gang stays on the ground, that only leaves two ... which means no more than four people could be in the race.'

Harold nodded.

'So we have to pick two from our gang and two from yours?'

Harold shook his head.

'What now?' Jonathan was getting exasperated.

'Billy and Mark aren't experienced climbers. We have to match ability too.'

Jonathan thought about this for a moment. 'That's ridiculous!' he burst out. 'If we take away Billy and Mark, there's only you left.'

'That's right.' Harold was looking at him carefully.

'So there'll only be two in the race?'

'Yes,' said Harold.

Jonathan sighed. 'OK, Harold. It's you on one side, then, and me on the other — and the rest on the ground, watching.'

Harold shook his head again. 'I want Mackey.'

Jonathan glared at him. 'I'm the leader of the Red Belly gang — you're the leader of the Yellow Belly gang. It's my place.'

'You're bigger than me,' countered Harold quickly.

'He's right,' agreed Mackey, delighted. 'Size has to be even too.'

Jonathan was speechless with rage, but he knew he'd been outsmarted.

'Sounds fair,' Felicity said. 'As long as you realise what you're taking on, Harold. Mackey is a brilliant climber.'

'So am I,' said Harold calmly. 'I've been practising.'

'That's it, then? All agreed?' Felicity checked around.

Everyone nodded. Jonathan was sulking, but he nodded too.

'We'll meet here, at the Captain's Table, tomorrow morning, ten o'clock.'

'Eleven o'clock,' corrected Harold. 'Billy and Mark have to come from the village.'

'Eleven o'clock it is, so,' said Felicity.

Harold smiled — a very satisfied smile.

UP THE RED BELLY

By half past nine the next morning, Mackey and Felicity were up at the very top of the Red Belly, sussing out the best route for the race. Mackey reckoned he could get a better idea of which way to go by viewing the woods from above. The top of the Red Belly was perfect for this.

The Red Belly was the tallest tree in the woods, towering over all the others. It was the oldest tree, too, with a massive trunk that was quite difficult to climb. Years ago, someone had daubed the trunk with a big circle of red paint, which gave the Red Belly its name.

Halfway up, the tree divided into a spread of thick branches, leaving a hollow where the gang could sit without being seen from below. They called this the Crow's Nest, and it was their headquarters. Jonathan was down there right now, entering plans for the race in their logbook. They also kept things hidden in little nooks and crannies around the Crow's Nest: Mackey's wrestling magazines, letters from Dara — a gang member who was living in Zambia — and sunflower seeds and raisins for survival rations, in case they were ever besieged.

Up at the very top of the tree, the branches thinned out and swayed alarmingly. But the view was worth the danger. Mackey and Felicity could see the sea, way off in the distance, and the city too. Inland, the airport straddled the horizon, and the gang often watched planes taking off and landing. Sometimes the planes flew right over the Red Belly, and the gang would shout and wave as they were deafened by the noise. But it was the church spire that really showed just how tall the Red Belly was: both were the same height.

They could see into all the back gardens on Conker Road, too. The gang lived in the middle houses, which had a lane behind them, and the Red Belly was visible from all their bedroom windows. Felicity never pulled her curtains at night; she liked to lie in bed and look at the dark shape of the Red Belly against the night sky. In the morning, the sun rose right behind it and hung in its branches like a big orange fruit.

'See-saw, Margery Daw ....' Mackey was acting the maggot as usual, making his branch sway so much that it finally crashed into Felicity's, almost dislodging her.

'Hey, watch it! Are you trying to kill me?' yelled Felicity, tightening her grip and hugging the branch to her chest.

'If not stupid, won't fall,' retorted Mackey, with a cheeky grin.

'With you around, not even the Swallows and the Amazons would have been safe,' Felicity scolded. 'Get on with it, will you!'

Mackey looked down. The green canopy of Conker Woods was far below. From up there, he could see clearly where the trees were thickest and where there were gaps — or where the trees thinned out so much that he was likely to have trouble getting from one to another.

'Look at that,' he said, pointing. 'The right side of the woods is best.'

Felicity looked. She'd never really noticed before that the trees were slightly thicker on the lane side. The other side of the woods opened out onto a huge field, where the haunted gate-lodge stood.

Felicity frowned. 'That depends,' she answered.

'Depends on what?'

'Depends on what kind of trees they are. It still mightn't be easy to get from one to the next if the branches aren't good.'

'If they're close together, that's enough for me,' Mackey declared. 'I can always jump if there's a gap.'

Felicity had no doubt he would. Mackey was fearless when he put his mind to it.

'It's going to be a bit awkward if Harold chooses the same route .... It'd really be better if you each took a separate side of the woods.'

'Doesn't matter,' Mackey said. 'He'd only get in my way at the very beginning. After that, I'll be ahead of him.'

'You're very sure of yourself,' laughed Felicity.

'Well ... me against Harold! It's no contest, is it?'

'Harold is tricky,' said Felicity. 'You should know that by now — remember last year?'

Mackey remembered. Harold had made complete fools out of them on more than one occasion. 'This is different,' he said defensively. 'It takes years to get really good at climbing — and Harold hasn't had that much practice.'

'Maybe he's been practising up drainpipes too,' laughed Felicity. That was how Mackey had learnt to climb, when he lived in a city pub.

Mackey decided he'd had enough of hearing about Harold. 'Let's go down,' he said.

They climbed down to the Crow's Nest. Jonathan was still writing laboriously in the logbook. Joan and Muggins had joined him; and, to their surprise, so had Orla.

'Hello, stranger,' Felicity greeted her. 'Didn't expect to see you here today.'

Orla was carefully examining her black-painted fingernails. 'Look!' she complained. 'I've chipped my polish climbing up.'

'True sacrifice to the cause,' sniggered Mackey.

'She's only here because Mum banned her from going up the village by herself,' Muggins revealed.

'She did not! I can go any time I like!'

'She said the gang had to go with you.'

'You'd think I was a child or something,' complained Orla. 'My mother can be *so* embarrassing, and illogical too — remember when she used to complain about all the time I spent in the woods?'

'That was only because she wanted you to stay in the garden and mind the little ones,' said Muggins.

'And I did, too, for years,' glowered Orla. 'She's never satisfied.'

'It's half past ten,' Joan observed suddenly. 'Shouldn't we be talking about the race?'

'I've been thinking about that,' said Jonathan. 'As I'm the race manager, tactics are really my job.'

'Race manager!' Mackey howled with laughter. Jonathan could be awfully pompous at times.

'When I'm up there,' Mackey explained, still laughing, 'I won't have time for instructions. It'll be *Go! go! go!*'

'I could run ahead a bit and tell you where the best route is.'

'Forget it!' Mackey was all business now. 'I don't want any distractions once I start.'

'Better lock up Columbus, then,' Jonathan said nastily. 'He'll probably bark his stupid head off, as usual.'

'Columbus is coming,' Mackey said firmly. 'He comes on all my adventures.'

There was a short silence as they let things simmer down a bit. Into the silence came a distant calling voice.

'Joan! ... Joanie!'

'Oh, no!' wailed Joan. 'Not now. I don't *believe* this!'

'Stinky-poo time,' laughed Mackey.

Joan clapped her hands to her ears, trying to blot

out the sound, as the call came again.

'Joa-nie!'

'He's useless! Completely useless! Can't he do any-thing by himself? Now he's going to make me miss the race.'

'Do what Jonathan does,' advised Felicity. 'Pretend you don't hear.'

'How can I?' railed Joan. 'He won't care, but Kevin will. Kevin is the one who'll suffer. He must be really bad .... I'll probably have to bath him. Oh, I'd better go ....' She swung herself over the edge of the Crow's Nest and climbed down the Red Belly. Then she was gone, across the clearing and into the woods towards home.

The gang were sympathetic. Joan's dad had taken a year's career break to stay at home and look after Kevin. It wasn't proving a great success — not from Joan's point of view, anyway.

'Remember when her da was away at sea?' Mackey said. 'She thought the sun, moon and stars shone out of his eyes.'

'That's because she hardly ever saw him,' Orla answered.

'And remember when Joan's granny lived with them, and she never had to lift a finger in the house?' said Felicity, who had always envied Joan such freedom.

'Well, she's sure making up for it now,' Mackey declared. 'Her da won't do anything, never mind change a dirty nappy. He just sits reading the paper and lets Joan do it all.'

'She should tell her mum,' Muggins advised. Joan's mum was a nurse and worked a lot of overtime.

'She doesn't want her mum to know,' Orla said. 'I don't blame her, after all the trouble last summer.'

When Joan's granny, Dorcas, had decided to move back to her own house, Joan's parents had argued for weeks over which of them should stay at home and mind the baby. The rows had been so bitter that Joan had become convinced that her parents were going to split up, like Mackey's folks had.

'If she tells her mum,' Orla went on, 'it'll start the rows again.'

'And her da might go away on a ship and never come back,' said Mackey. That was what Joan had been afraid of, the year before, and Mackey had managed to get himself mixed up in the whole affair. 'At least this time she can't blame me,' he added fervently.

The conversation was suddenly interrupted by a warning growl from below. Mackey looked over the edge of the Crow's Nest. Columbus had been asleep at the foot of the Red Belly, but now he was awake and growling at a boxer dog who was trying to be friendly.

'It's Arnie,' Mackey reported. 'Harold must be ready.'

'Let's get down out of here, then,' said Orla, swinging over the side of the Crow's Nest.

'Just let me at him!' Mackey grinned. 'Yellow Bellies, here we come!'

They spotted Harold heading towards the bottom of the woods with his gang. Columbus and Arnie were now frolicking in and out through the trees, the best of pals.

'Hey, hang on!' Felicity yelled after Harold. 'I thought we arranged to meet at the Captain's Table.'

The Yellow Bellies stopped and waited for the Red Bellies to catch up.

'You weren't there on time,' said Harold.

'It's only eleven now,' Felicity protested.

'Three minutes past,' Harold said. 'I don't like waiting around.'

'Hope you're ready to be trounced,' Mackey jeered.

'Big mouth, small brain,' Harold answered. Billy and Mark giggled and looked at Mackey.

'I see you've brought along Giggle and Gawk.' Mackey was being nasty.

'Their names are Billy and Mark,' said Harold with a dangerous calm.

'Giggle and Gawk,' Mackey said deliberately.

'Oh, cut it out, Mackey!' snapped Orla. 'You can be so juvenile.'

'I'm glad somebody agrees with me,' Harold said.

Mackey glared at Orla. 'Whose side are you on, anyway?'

But Orla had slipped off one of her shoes and was busy examining her black-painted toenails.

Mackey lost interest. 'Let's get on with it,' he said. He walked ahead, leaving the others to follow.

There was a wall at the bottom of the woods which

was the boundary of an old estate. Though the trees there were extremely thick, they weren't good climbing trees. Many of them were weedy-looking, without good solid branches. The start of the race was going to be difficult, and both Mackey and Harold knew it. They were examining the ceiling of trees overhead, sizing up the problem.

'We can each start from a different side of the woods,' Mackey suggested. 'It'll stop us from bumping into each other.'

'Good idea,' said Harold.

'So I'll start from here and you can start from the field side.'

'No, *I'll* start from here and *you* start from the field side.'

'But I'm starting from here,' insisted Mackey.

'So am I,' said Harold firmly.

'Right,' growled Mackey, 'only don't blame me if you get knocked down in the rush.'

Harold just smiled.

'We'll say "Ready, steady, go",' Jonathan suggested, looking at Billy and Mark. 'If we all say it together then nobody can claim the start wasn't fair.'

Billy and Mark nodded agreement.

'OK. On your marks ....'

'Ready!

'Steady!

'*Go!*'

Mackey and Harold both dived for the same tree. Mackey elbowed Harold in the face and got ahead, but Harold was close on his heels. The two gangs watched with apprehension.

Halfway up, while Mackey was still climbing, Harold took a flying leap into the next tree.

'He's ahead! He's ahead!' Billy and Mark shrieked, beside themselves with excitement. Mackey, realising

his mistake, swung out onto the end of a branch and recklessly launched himself into the air. He fell a heart-stopping distance before he managed to grab a branch of the next tree. But Harold was still ahead. Billy and Mark ran below, cheering him on. 'Come on, Harold! Come on!'

'Go for it, Mackey!' yelled the Red Belly gang. 'Get him! Get him!'

Columbus had spotted Mackey up the tree. He started yapping wildly. Arnie, unable to figure out what was going on, ran around frantically, stopping every now and then with a puzzled look on his crumpled little face.

The two boys were travelling at quite a pace. Mackey, determined to catch up with Harold, became totally reckless, flinging himself from branch to branch like a monkey. Harold was being more careful, but he was fast and sure.

'How did Harold get so good?' Felicity asked in awe. It seemed only yesterday that Harold had been this annoying little kid from across the road whose mother wouldn't even let him go out of the garden, never mind climb a tree.

'He's intelligent,' Orla said. 'It takes intelligence to be a good climber.'

'Then we're really intelligent,' declared Muggins happily.

'I can't believe how good he is!' Jonathan had his eyes firmly fixed on Harold. 'I wish Mackey'd get on with it!'

'He will,' said Felicity. 'You know Mackey — he won't let anyone beat him .... Look, he's caught up!'

The two climbers were neck and neck, fighting for the same branches. The gangs watched anxiously from below.

'Get out of my way, kid!' they heard Mackey yell, as

he attempted to pass Harold.

'*You* get out of *my* way!' Harold yelled back.

Mackey grabbed an overhead branch, then swung himself right over Harold's head and into the next tree. The Red Belly gang cheered wildly. 'Come on, Mackey! Come on!'

'Yap-yap-yap!' Columbus barked, throwing himself ecstatically at the trunk of the tree, trying to get up to Mackey. Arnie, totally confused, was going around in circles and snapping at his stumpy little tail.

Billy and Mark kept their eyes glued to Harold as he followed Mackey. The two racers had travelled nearly halfway up the woods and were at the edge of the Red Belly clearing. Mackey should have had the advantage, being so familiar with the trees; but Harold, responding quickly to the improved climbing conditions, was in his element. By the time they'd left the clearing behind, Harold had caught up again.

They worked their way up the woods, towards the Captain's Table, neck and neck the whole way. The race was going to be a close thing, if it didn't end in a complete draw.

'They're really well matched,' Felicity said.

'I think Mackey'll win, all the same,' said Jonathan confidently.

'That kid is amazing!' Orla, completely involved with the race now, was watching Harold.

'Come *on*, Mackey!' screamed Muggins.

Billy and Mark had started up a chant: 'Yellow Belly, Yellow Belly, Yellow Belly ....'

They came to the edge of the Yellow Belly clearing. This was Harold's territory; but it had belonged to the Red Belly gang first, so the trees were equally familiar to them. Mackey and Harold fought each other all the way around, neither one gaining on the other.

Then they were into the top section of the woods,

going up towards the Tunnel. It was difficult territory for the gang members on the ground, as the whole area was full of thick bushes. They kept to the path that ran along by the ditch, so they were to one side of the climbers rather than directly underneath them. The dogs had disappeared.

The climbing was harder here, too. At one point, as the trees thinned out, Harold got completely stuck with nowhere to go, and had to backtrack to a better position. But Mackey was finding it difficult too; he was constantly having to slow down and check the route ahead to avoid the same fate.

Jonathan tried to be helpful. 'To the left, Mackey!' he shouted. 'To the left!'

'That's not allowed,' Harold protested. 'No help from the ground!'

'Left, Mackey, left!' yelled Jonathan, ignoring Harold.

'Shut up, will ya!' Mackey screamed furiously. 'I don't need your help.'

They weren't far from the top of the woods, and the end of the race was in sight.

Suddenly, a fearsome yelping and snarling rent the woods behind them. They all froze, listening — climbers and followers alike. A high, piercing wail was drowned out by frenzied howling, and someone was screaming ... screaming ....

The screams came closer.

Joan appeared on the path, utterly hysterical.

'Mackey! Mackey! Columbus is killing Arnie! He's covered in blood .... Oh, come quick! Quick!'

Mackey dropped out of the tree as if he'd been shot. He landed in a perfect parachute roll and was already running as he got to his feet.

Harold took a bit longer to get down, tumbling from branch to branch and landing awkwardly from the final drop. He was limping when he got up, but he took off at quite a pace, hopping along as if his life depended on it. The rest of them, snapping out of their shock, ran after him.

When they reached the Red Belly clearing, Mackey and Harold were already trying to separate the two dogs. Arnie was pinned against the trunk of the Red Belly, howling. Columbus had him by the ear, snarling ferociously. Both dogs were splattered with blood. Joan was wailing like a banshee.

Harold thumped Columbus frantically on the nose, trying to make him let go. Columbus only growled louder.

'Get them away from the tree!' screamed Mackey. 'Away — from the — *tree!*'

Harold pulled Arnie by the collar, and Mackey hauled Columbus backwards. They dragged the two dogs, still locked together, out into the middle of the clearing.

Columbus stopped growling, rolled his eyes, then let Arnie go. He stood there, tongue hanging out, panting heavily.

Arnie looked pathetic. Blood was pouring steadily from a nasty tear in his ear. Harold dropped to his knees and hugged the big boxer, almost crying. 'Oh, Arnie .... It's all right. It's all right! I'll look after you now.' He turned angrily to Mackey. 'That dog of yours is vicious.'

'Columbus is *not* vicious,' Mackey protested. 'He was just defending what's his. Arnie was sitting right on top of that rat he buried yesterday.'

'What!'

'I don't believe this,' groaned Jonathan.

'That's disgusting!' Joan declared. 'You mean you let him bury a rat under our tree?'

'I didn't *let* him,' Mackey protested. 'He just did it.'

Harold leaned his cheek against Arnie's soft fur for

a moment, then sighed. 'I'd better get Arnie home, he's going to need the vet. Come on, boy!' Arnie, battle-scarred as he was, came to heel and followed Harold out of the clearing.

Billy and Mark silently trotted after them.

☆   ☆   ☆

Later that afternoon, the Red Belly gang were gathered around the Captain's Table. Mackey was angry and defensive.

'It wasn't Columbus's fault. Anyway, Arnie's not badly injured — he only had four stitches in his ear. He just bled a lot.'

'What did Harold's mother say?' Felicity asked.

'I dunno,' said Mackey, 'but my ma was rightly mad. She had to pay for the vet.'

'Is she stopping your pocket money?' Muggins enquired curiously.

'Might as well,' Mackey growled. 'She takes half of it anyway. I'm still paying for Mr Finnerty's glasshouse from last year.'

'I know how you feel,' said Felicity. 'I went a whole summer without any pocket money. It was just one thing after another.'

'Do you think Harold will run the race again?' Jonathan asked.

'Shouldn't have to,' Mackey protested. 'I was winning anyway.'

'It was anybody's race, really,' Orla said. 'Harold could easily have got ahead again. Besides, it was your fault the race was stopped.'

'No it wasn't!'

'You'd better get rid of the rat,' declared Joan. 'Otherwise that crazy dog of yours is going to attack one of us sooner or later.'

'He won't.' Mackey didn't sound very convincing.

'Promise!' Joan persisted. 'Promise you'll get rid of it. I'm not going near the Red Belly again until you do.'

'OK! OK!' Mackey was fed up with the whole business.

'We'll ask Harold if he'll race again tomorrow,' Jonathan decided. 'The sooner we get this settled, the better. We don't want another summer of fighting — do we?'

They did not.

'I want a nice quiet summer for once,' Joan declared.

'It'll have to be in the afternoon,' Felicity reminded Jonathan. 'Tomorrow's Wednesday; it's our day for doing old Fitzy's garden.'

'Right,' said Jonathan, 'afternoon it is. Everyone agree?'

Everyone agreed.

What they didn't know then was that the race would never be run. The battle for the Captain's Table would be forgotten.

Things were about to happen which would turn their whole world upside down and threaten to change Conker Woods forever ....

Interesting Business

Wednesday morning saw them all knocking on Mr Fitzhenry's door at nine o'clock, as usual. Mr Fitzhenry lived six doors up from the laneway. He had a long garden which backed straight onto the woods.

He was an old foe of the gang's. They'd had many a run-in with him in the past, over his gooseberry bushes. The ripe fruit was irresistible to the gang, and they raided the bushes each summer. But old Fitzy had suffered a stroke, two winters before, which had left him in poor health. His garden, which he'd always been so proud of, had become completely overgrown. Then, last summer, Felicity and Jonathan's mother had come up with a brilliant idea: the gang should help him out.

They had protested in vain. In fact, they had been terrified at the idea of facing old Fitzy — but they could hardly explain their reluctance to Mrs Kelly. So they'd ended up spending every Wednesday of their summer holidays in Mr Fitzhenry's garden, wrestling with a whole year's overgrowth. It had been hard work, and they'd had some very nasty moments with old Fitzy in the beginning.

Now it wasn't so bad. They only did one morning a week, as they'd been coming in on Saturdays for most of the winter to give the place a quick tidy-up. The garden was in fine shape. It was just a matter of keeping it that way.

Mrs Finnerty answered the door and showed the gang through to the kitchen. Mrs Finnerty lived across the lane from the Kellys' house. She had once been an enemy of the gang's too, but now she was busy being old Fitzy's home help and hadn't the time to bother them much any more.

'Hi, Mr Fitzhenry! Hi, Tiggy! Hi, Scut!' The gang shouted their greetings as they emerged into the back garden. Old Fitzy was sitting in an armchair on the garden path. He nodded in return. Tiggy and Scut went wild, running around and barking, and coming back to lick each and every one of the gang. Mackey had brought Columbus along, too. Tiggy was Columbus's mother and Scut was his brother — they'd been born at the same time.

Felicity remembered how jealous she'd been when old Fitzy had given the puppy to Mackey — because Mackey's dog, Boozer, had just died. Boozer was now buried under the cherry tree by Mackey's back gate. Felicity had been pleading with her mother for months to let her have a dog of her own. Mrs Kelly always said no — she didn't want a dog, and there was Mrs Durkin to consider. Mrs Durkin looked after the house when Mrs Kelly was at work. She was a wizard at housework, so much so that Jonathan had nicknamed her 'Scrub-Scrub'. But Mrs Durkin didn't like anything that caused dirt, like children ... or dogs.

In spite of this, Felicity had set her heart on Scut, but old Fitzy had refused to part with him. So, instead, at her mother's suggestion, Felicity had taken on the responsibility of walking Tiggy and Scut every day, and had learnt how to look after them. Mackey came on the walks too, sometimes, so Columbus could be with his family.

The gang got the lawnmower and shears and edging-clippers out of the shed and set to work. They were used to the routine by now.

Mr Fitzhenry had been unwell again that winter,

and he was more unpredictable than ever. Sometimes he wouldn't talk to them. Other days he was all chat and reminiscences about his years in Africa.

Today he was grumpy. 'Don't let that dog dig up my garden,' he said sharply to Mackey.

'He belongs here,' protested Mackey indignantly. 'It's his home.'

'Doesn't mean he can do what he likes.'

'It's natural for dogs to dig!'

'Not in my garden,' said Mr Fitzhenry firmly.

Mackey turned away and made a face. The rest of the gang giggled. Old Fitzy had a poor opinion of the way Mackey was bringing up Columbus, and constantly made the fact known.

Things were better when Joan brought Kevin along, as old Fitzy was fascinated by the little fellow. But Joan was late this morning. The gang had been at work for about half an hour before they heard Mrs Finnerty letting her through to the back. She had the buggy with her.

When Mr Fitzhenry saw Kevin, his face lit up. He had eyes only for the child. Joan unstrapped Kevin from the buggy and he tottered over to old Fitzy at once. He clutched at the old man's trousers to stop himself from falling, and Mr Fitzhenry beamed. It was still weird to see old Fitzy smiling — his smile had been unused for so long.

The gang got on with their work. They had learnt that the quicker they did it, the sooner they would be free. Sometimes they were finished by twelve o'clock.

At half past ten, Mrs Finnerty brought them out glasses of lemonade and biscuits.

'The catering sure has improved around here,' hissed Mackey, as they sat down on the grass for a break.

'Remember the first time?' Felicity giggled.

'Bread and water,' Muggins mumbled, his mouth full of biscuit.

'Prison food,' said Mackey. 'And a guard dog, too!'

'I was terrified that day,' Joan admitted.

'At least we don't have to cut the grass with nail scissors now,' Orla said, examining her long black fingernails. She'd been using the lawnmower, and her varnish was still intact. 'Not a single chip,' she declared with satisfaction.

'I don't know why you want to put that stuff on your nails anyway,' Mackey said.

'It's different,' Orla replied. 'At least it's not boring. Everything gets so boring, boring, boring!'

Mackey stared at her. Orla had gone beyond understanding.

'Your hair looks like the grass did last year when we cut it with nail scissors.' Joan was examining Orla's haircut close up.

'Good, isn't it?' Orla agreed happily.

'What did your mum say when you did that?'

'She went mad, but she couldn't do anything about it. I did offer to shave the lot off, so it would be neater — but she went twice as mad. There's no pleasing parents at all.' Orla gave a big, dramatic sigh.

'You're only finding that out now?' Mackey retorted.

Jonathan looked at his watch. 'Let's get back to work. We'll finish nice and early today.'

'I'm not doing any weeding,' Orla said. 'It wrecks my nails.'

'You can sweep up,' Felicity suggested.

'The lupins are all withered.' Muggins was examining a dead flower-head. 'Old Fitzy says if I cut these off, the lupins will flower again in August.'

'That's so they won't use up all their energy making seed-pods,' Mackey said knowledgeably. Mr Fitzhenry had taught them quite a bit about gardening since the year before. 'I'm dying for the red-hot pokers to come into bloom again — they're my favourites.'

'I thought your favourites were hollyhocks,' Joan said.

'I've changed my mind.' Mackey grinned and went to check on Columbus, who had gone down to the fruit garden behind the big hedge.

The three dogs were playing around the gooseberry bushes, and Columbus hadn't been digging at all.

'Good dog!' Mackey told him, pleased. He hated it when old Fitzy started lecturing.

The gang were finished with the garden by a quarter past twelve. They put the gardening things away in the shed and got ready to go.

'Is it all right if I take Tiggy and Scut for their walk now, Mr Fitzhenry?' Felicity asked.

Old Fitzy nodded. He was busy waving goodbye to Kevin as Joan strapped the child into the buggy.

'Bye, Mr Fitzhenry!'

'See you next week.'

'Come on, Columbus .... It's OK, Tiggy's coming too.' Mackey grabbed Columbus's collar as he tried to belt down the garden again.

They went through the house and out the front door onto Conker Road.

'See you after lunch,' Felicity said to Joan and Orla and Muggins. 'Mackey and me are going to walk the dogs down to the old estate for a bit.'

'Let's all meet at two o'clock,' Jonathan suggested, 'up the Red Belly.'

☆　　☆　　☆

Later, they sat in the Crow's Nest and discussed the business of the Captain's Table. They could hear shouting and laughter coming from Harold's end of the woods.

'He's in a good humour, anyway,' Jonathan observed.

'Let's sort things out for once and for all,' said Joan firmly. 'We're not going to start fighting again.'

'Felicity should talk to Harold,' Muggins said. 'He likes her.'

Jonathan shook his head. 'Mackey's the one who has to race — he should negotiate.'

'I thought you were race manager,' Mackey observed. 'Isn't that what race managers are for?'

'Well ... OK, I'll do it if you like.' Jonathan looked pleased.

'Hurry up, will you!' Orla called from below. She had refused to climb the Red Belly, claiming it wrecked her nails.

'We're coming!' shouted Felicity.

'Let's go,' Mackey said.

The gang slipped out of the Crow's Nest, one by one, and joined Orla in the clearing. Together they set off up the woods. Mackey had left Columbus at home, in case Arnie was around. His mother thought it would be better for Columbus to lie low for a day or two.

Harold and his gang were up the Yellow Belly. They could all be seen, as their headquarters weren't as private as the Crow's Nest. Across the clearing, the Captain's Table still had its warning note attached.

Jonathan stood below the Yellow Belly.

'Harold!' he called.

Harold and Billy and Mark stared down at him.

'What do you want?' Harold's tone was belligerent.

'We want to arrange a new time for the race.'

'There won't be another race.'

'What about the Captain's Table?'

'It's mine!'

'But ... can't we at least share it? You suggested that yourself.'

'I've changed my mind.'

'Harold, be reasonable,' Jonathan pleaded.

'Go away!' said Harold. 'You're disturbing us.'

'Want us to disturb you some more?' threatened

Mackey, stepping in beside Jonathan.

'Mackey!' warned Felicity. 'Don't start!'

Harold leaned forward.

'I'm only going to explain this once,' he said, with an icy calm. 'You can't share the Captain's Table because that's where Arnie sits when we're up here. Since nobody seems to be in control of Columbus, I'm not having him here fighting every day. Keep away, the lot of you!'

'I don't see Arnie on the Captain's Table now,' Mackey snorted.

'That's because he's at home, recovering from a vicious, unprovoked attack. The Captain's Table is mine — and that's final.'

Mackey knew when he was beaten. 'Who wants the stupid thing, anyway?' he yelled. 'Keep it! Come on, gang, we've more interesting business to discuss.' He turned and walked away at such a pace that the others had to run to catch up with him.

He led them out into the field behind the woods, where they lay down in the long grass.

'You've blown it rightly now!' Jonathan said to Mackey. 'You should have left things to me.'

Mackey glowered. 'Stupid little kid — we should never have let him into the woods in the first place.'

'What's the more interesting business we have to discuss?' Muggins asked hopefully.

'Are you dense or something?' said Mackey shortly.

Muggins looked so hurt that Felicity took pity on him. 'Mackey only said that to save face,' she explained. 'We don't really have interesting business to discuss.'

'Oh!' Muggins said. Then he added brightly, 'We could discuss the haunted gate-lodge. That's interesting.'

They all laughed, breaking the tension.

'Not a bad idea,' Mackey said, sitting up and staring across the field at the gate-lodge. 'I've always had a mind to break in there again.'

'Do you think the ghost is really gone?' asked Joan.

'Should be,' Felicity said, 'after what we did last year.'

The gate-lodge was haunted by the ghost of a man who had hanged himself there. The doors and windows were all bricked up, but it had once had a hole in the back wall where the gang could gain entrance. They had slept there one night, the previous summer, hoping to meet the ghost. Their night of adventure had ended in pure terror, and Mr Kelly — Jonathan and Felicity's father — had threatened the County Council with legal action unless the gate-lodge was made secure. The council workers had come the next day and sealed off the opening.

But the gang hadn't forgotten about the ghost, and a chance remark by Dara had set them thinking. Dara lived in Zambia, but he'd been home on a visit that summer, staying with his granny in the village. Dara had said that tribes in Africa believed that dawn was the gateway between worlds.

Felicity, thinking about that, had figured their ghost was trapped in this life because he couldn't find the gates of dawn to pass into the next. So, the night of their sleep-out under the Red Belly, the gang had held a ceremony at dawn to see their ghost safely on his way. They didn't know if it had worked, but they had intended to find out.

'I might come back tomorrow with a hammer,' Mackey said, suddenly all enthusiastic. 'We could bang a hole in the wall and sleep there again some night.'

'You're joking!' Joan screeched. 'Haven't you had enough of that?' Mackey had slept there twice already, once on his own.

'No,' said Mackey, 'I haven't.' He grinned. 'I'm going to explore this *very* interesting business first thing in the morning. Anyone want to join me?'

A Big Shock

Mackey came tearing up Conker Lane the next morning in a right panic.

Felicity and Jonathan were just coming out of their side gate.

'The gate-lodge!' screamed Mackey. 'They're knocking down the haunted gate-lodge! Come quickly!'

'Hold on a sec,' Jonathan said, grabbing Mackey by the arm. 'Who's knocking down the gate-lodge?'

'I don't know. I don't know what's happening. Oh, come on! We have to stop it!'

Mackey struggled free from Jonathan's grasp and went racing away down the lane. Felicity and Jonathan followed. They rounded the corner into the back part of the lane, which ran along the edge of Conker Woods.

Joan was just coming out her garden gate, having heard the commotion.

'What's up?' she asked.

Mackey was dancing around the place, unable to keep still. 'The haunted gate-lodge — they're knocking it down. We have to stop them. Get the others!'

'I'll get Orla and Muggins,' Felicity offered, and she ran towards the Duggans' back gate.

The Duggans' garden was filled with kids and toys, as usual. Carly, who was nearly seven, and Conor, who was just six, were trying to do handstands on the grass — not very successfully. Shane, who was four, was swinging from a sheet on the line. Aisling, two and a half, was eating clay. Felicity knocked on the Duggans' back door. Mrs Duggan answered it.

'Mrs Duggan,' Felicity blurted out breathlessly, 'I need Orla and Muggins urgently. It's an emergency.'

Mrs Duggan stared at her, amused. 'I suppose this is a new ploy to get them out of doing their jobs,' she said.

'No, it's not, Mrs Duggan .... Please — just this once? It's really, really important.'

'Oh, go on with you, then!' sighed Mrs Duggan. She turned into the kitchen and shouted, 'Orla! Michael! You're wanted.'

Orla and Muggins came running. When they realised their mother was giving them permission to go, they took off at top speed, dragging Felicity with them.

'Come on,' Orla hissed, 'before she changes her mind! Thanks for coming to the rescue, Felicity. She nabbed me this morning and said I was jolly well going to help, whether I liked it or not.'

'How did you get her to agree?' Muggins asked. 'I've only half my jobs done.'

They went down the garden and out the back gate, latching it firmly so the little Duggans couldn't follow. The others were waiting impatiently in the lane. Joan had managed to calm Mackey down.

'What's this all about?' Orla finally asked. She'd been so glad to get away from the house that she hadn't even enquired.

Mackey explained. Orla and Muggins were just as taken aback as the rest of the gang.

'It must be the County Council,' Orla said. 'That's who Mr Kelly complained to last summer.'

Mackey looked accusingly at Jonathan and Felicity. 'Your da hasn't been making trouble again, has he?'

'No, he has not!' Jonathan protested.

'Well, somebody must have been on to the Council,' Orla said. 'Why else would they be here?'

'Maybe it's not the Council,' Mackey said darkly. 'Maybe it's just thieves pinching stuff.'

'I've heard of things like that,' Muggins exclaimed. 'A removal van pulls into the driveway of a house and takes all the furniture, and everybody thinks it's OK, that people are moving house. Only it turns out to be thieves.'

'Well, they're not getting our gate-lodge,' Mackey said. 'Come on, gang — to the rescue!'

Into Conker Woods they went. The morning sun shone down through the trees, speckling the floor of the woods with pink and gold light. It was like a great cathedral, Felicity always thought, with trunks for pillars and leaf-filtered light for stained glass. The ground underfoot was brown and loamy and smelt of secret summer places. In silence they filed through to the other side of the woods and emerged into the field beyond.

They stood and gaped in dismay.

'The roof's gone!' Felicity cried. 'The roof's gone already.'

'I know,' fumed Mackey. 'That's what I was trying to tell you.'

'They must have been here at the crack of dawn to get so much done,' Orla exclaimed.

'They're sneaky,' agreed Jonathan. 'Tried to do it before anyone noticed.'

'But they can't!' Muggins wailed.

'They just have,' said Mackey grimly. 'Come on. Let's tackle them!'

He led the way across the field towards the gate-lodge — or what was left of it. The roof-beams lay on the ground, a pile of grey slates beside them. Work had already started on dismantling the walls. The stones were being carefully placed in a waiting lorry. The exposed chimney-stack rose up behind the workmen, stark and bare.

Mackey strode up angrily, the gang following behind.

'What d'ya think you're doing?' he shouted. 'That's our gate-lodge!'

The men stopped work in surprise, then grinned when they saw Mackey stomping around below them in the long grass.

'Not any more, it isn't,' one of them laughed.

At that moment, a huge man came tearing around from the back of the building. He looked about seven feet tall and was built like a battleship.

'Clear off!' he yelled, shaking a fist at the gang. 'Clear off outa here!'

'And who d'ya think you are?' Mackey asked cheekily.

'The foreman, that's who I am,' the man said, a dangerous tone in his voice.

Felicity stepped forward. 'Please, mister, we only want to know what's going on.'

'Demolition. That's what's going on.' The foreman was slightly mollified by Felicity's polite tone. 'It's no place for kids. You get hurt — I get blamed. That's the way it works. Now shift yourselves!'

'But why?' Felicity persisted. 'Why are you knocking it down?'

'Go ask the County Council,' barked the foreman. 'Now *shift*!' His final roar sent the gang hurrying back across the field.

They sat by the edge of Conker Woods and watched.

'They're saving all the stones,' Felicity said. 'Maybe they're going to rebuild the lodge somewhere else.'

'Where?' asked Muggins.

'I don't know,' answered Felicity. 'Just somewhere.'

'But why would they bother to take it down, after all these years?' Jonathan wondered.

'Well, your da threatened them with legal action, didn't he?'

'That's not fair!' protested Jonathan. 'You can't blame us for that. If my dad hadn't complained, your mum would have. My dad was doing it on behalf of all the parents.'

'Still and all,' Mackey said accusingly, 'he was the one who made the phone call.'

'You really don't think that's the reason, do you?' Felicity asked.

'Why else?' Mackey shrugged his shoulders.

Felicity didn't answer. She was appalled. Surely she and Jonathan weren't going to get the blame for all of this?

Orla yawned and lay back, sunning herself.

'I don't know why we're all so sorry, anyway,' Joan suddenly declared. 'It was a horrible place — dark and horrible!' She shivered.

'It was scary,' Mackey said. 'It was one of the scariest places I've ever been.'

'What happens if the ghost isn't really gone?' Muggins asked fearfully, looking at the roofless shell.

'He should be,' said Felicity firmly.

'If he's not gone,' Muggins persisted, 'will he get out now that there's no roof?'

'Yeah, Muggins ... he's coming to take you away, ha-ha!' Mackey made his hands into claws and pulled his mouth wide with his thumbs, in a ferocious grimace.

'Stoppit!' wailed Muggins. 'It's not funny. If the ghost gets out, maybe he'll come and haunt Conker Woods.'

'*Boo!*' shouted Mackey, making them all jump. It was astonishing how even talking about the ghost still had the power to unnerve them.

'Look,' said Joan, 'the foreman's going off.'

Sure enough, the foreman was climbing into his car. He started the engine, then swung the car around in a circle and went bumping over the grass towards the breach in the top wall that led to the main road.

'The men have stopped work,' Jonathan exclaimed.

'Let's go talk to them.' In an instant, Mackey was on

his feet and running across the field. The others trooped after him.

When they reached the gate-lodge, they found that Mackey had gone around to the back. He was talking to three workmen. Two of the men were quite old — one had white hair, and the other was bald but had a beard; the third man was younger and had his hair tied back in a ponytail. They were making tea, pouring water from a big kettle that had been boiling on a gas stove. They didn't seem to mind the gang being there; in fact, they offered them Kimberley biscuits. The gang sat on the grass and picked at the marshmallow.

'Pity Columbus isn't here,' Mackey said. 'Kimberleys are his favourites.'

'You shouldn't be feeding him things like that,' Joan reproved him. 'They're bad for dogs.'

Mackey made a face at her and turned towards the workmen. 'Are you building the gate-lodge somewhere else?' he asked.

The men shook their heads.

'What are you doing with the stones, then?'

'Nice bit of cut stone, that,' said the bearded man. 'You won't get the like nowadays. Plenty'll buy it.'

Felicity could contain herself no longer. 'But why are you knocking it down at all?'

The men looked surprised.

'To make way for the new road, of course,' said the one with the ponytail.

'What road?'

'The one that's going to be built in this field.'

'Why would anyone want to put a road in an empty field?' Mackey asked, astonished.

'For the Old People's Home.'

'*What* Old People's Home?'

'The one that's going to be built here,' the man said patiently.

The gang were speechless. It couldn't be true! It couldn't possibly be true!

'You're taking our field?' Mackey bawled in outrage.

The workmen laughed.

'It's not your field, laddie,' said the white-haired man kindly. 'It belongs to the County Council, and they're the ones who are building the Old People's Home — or Senior Citizens' Retirement Home, as they prefer to call it nowadays.'

'But why haven't we heard about it?' Jonathan asked.

'Don't read the papers, do you?' said the white-haired man. 'No, I thought not. Planning notices were in all the papers, way back last year.'

The gang were silent, stunned, disbelieving.

The men finished their break, shaking the last of the tea out of their mugs before rinsing them with water from the big kettle.

'You kids had better scram before the foreman gets back,' said the bearded man. 'He'll skin you alive if he finds you here.'

The gang got up to go. They all looked miserable.

'Thanks, misters,' said Felicity, remembering her manners. 'And thanks for telling us.'

They heard the loud revving of an engine as the foreman's car came bumping through the gap in the wall.

The gang ran for their lives.

A Sad Farewell

Felicity tackled her mother about the gate-lodge that afternoon. Scrub-Scrub had gone home, and the house was quiet. Mrs Kelly was just in from work. She was having a cup of tea in the kitchen, completely absorbed in the big computer manual which was balanced on her lap.

'Mum,' Felicity began, 'they're knocking down the haunted gate-lodge.'

'That's nice.'

'Mum! You never even heard what I said!'

'I'm listening. Everything all right, love?' Mrs Kelly was not listening. She had her finger on a piece of text and was frowning with concentration.

Felicity tried again. 'They're building a road through our field.'

'Mmm ....'

'And an Old People's Home ....' Felicity stopped, to see if her mother would comment, then went on, 'It's going to have a flat roof so flying saucers can land and Martians can come and visit.'

'Mmm .... That's nice, love.'

Felicity gave up. It was useless talking to her mother when she was like that.

She tried it with her father at dinner.

'Dad, they're knocking down the haunted gate-lodge.'

Mr Kelly's fork was arrested in mid-air, cabbage dangling from its prongs, as he took in this astonishing statement.

'Best news I've had today,' he declared, and popped the cabbage into his mouth, chewing happily.

'It's not good news,' Jonathan protested. 'Why does everybody have to spoil our fun?'

'Nobody's spoiling your fun,' Mr Kelly said firmly. 'That lodge was a danger to every child in the area. It should have been removed years ago.'

'Did you phone the Council again, Dad?' Felicity asked apprehensively.

Mr Kelly looked at her questioningly. 'I phoned them last year.'

'But I mean now, this year.'

'No, I didn't ... but I might have done if there had been any more trouble.'

Felicity sighed with relief. At least that was something.

'Dad, did you know they were going to take our field?' Jonathan demanded. 'They want to build some stupid Old People's Home. It's not fair!'

Mr Kelly put down his knife and fork, glancing briefly across at Mrs Kelly before saying gently, 'It's not your field. Never was. It belongs to the County Council. You're lucky to have enjoyed it all these years.'

'Did you know about the Home?' Jonathan persisted.

'The planning application was in the papers last year,' Mr Kelly said, 'but I didn't know how quickly they were going to build. It might have taken years — then you'd all have been too grown-up to play there anyway.'

'Carly wouldn't,' Felicity protested. 'Nor would Shane, or Conor, or Kevin, or Aisling. Now there'll be nothing for them when they get bigger.'

Mrs Kelly was getting irritated. 'For heaven's sake, Felicity! Stop being so dramatic.'

Felicity glared at her mother. 'You're always on about keeping the world right for future generations.

51

Don't the future generations of Conker Road matter?'

'Of course they do,' Mrs Kelly said. 'But haven't you still got the woods? There are plenty of children who would give anything to have a place like that. You don't know how lucky you are. Now stop whinging about losing a bit of a field. Old people have to have somewhere to go too.'

'Why can't their families look after them?'

'Yeah,' broke in Jonathan, 'why can't they?'

Mr and Mrs Kelly looked at each other again. Mr Kelly raised his eyes to heaven.

'Mr Fitzhenry doesn't need an Old People's Home,' Felicity persisted. 'He's not even well, and he's perfectly independent — he just needs a bit of help from neighbours.'

'It's not quite that simple ....' Mrs Kelly began.

'Yes it is,' Felicity insisted. 'You said so yourself, last summer, when you made us go and do his garden.'

But Mr Kelly had had enough of arguments. 'Do you think we could have a bit of peace now to eat our dinner?'

Jonathan dug into his shepherd's pie and lifted a huge piece of crispy crust to his mouth.

Felicity put down her knife and fork. There was a hard lump of anger in her throat, and she couldn't eat a single bite.

☆   ☆   ☆

The next afternoon, the gang sat in the field and watched the rest of the gate-lodge vanish.

'Bye-bye, gate-lodge,' Felicity said softly to herself. The speed at which it had been dismantled was astounding. There were only a couple of rows of stonework left. Most of the stuff had already been carted away on the lorry.

Muggins was still talking about the ghost. He

couldn't seem to drop the subject.

'Look, he's gone,' Joan said, exasperated. 'Will you shut up about him!'

'Yes, but if he hasn't — if he's still here — would he go away on the lorry with the stones, or would he stay on the spot where the lodge used to be?'

'Muggins! You're getting complicated again,' Orla laughed.

'No he's not.' Mackey got all interested. 'That's a good question.'

'He'd go with the stones,' Jonathan said, 'and haunt the lodge when it's rebuilt.'

'Who says they're going to build another house with the stones?' Joan pointed out. 'They might just build a wall.'

'Then the ghost would haunt the wall — he'd sit up there like Humpty Dumpty,' Jonathan reckoned.

'No he wouldn't!' Mackey protested. 'A ghost is attached to a place. Even with the lodge gone, he'd still be here.' Mackey started to laugh. 'Hey, just imagine — when they build the new road and cars come up here at night, they'll see this skeleton hanging in mid-air. Bet there'll be lots of crashes.'

'That's not very nice, Mackey!' Joan reproved him.

'Might be true all the same.'

'Maybe the old people will be frightened and refuse to come and live here,' Jonathan said.

'It'll be too late for us then, anyway,' sighed Felicity. 'Once the Home is built, it's built. It won't make any difference whether people are frightened or not.'

'I'm glad we still have Conker Woods,' Mackey said. 'At least they can't take that.'

They were all silent as they stared at the workmen, who were starting on the very last row of stonework.

'Joanie .... Oh, Joa-nie!'

The call came floating through Conker Woods to

where they were sitting. Mackey sniggered.

Joan sighed and got up. She looked across at Mackey. 'You're coming with me this time,' she informed him.

'Who, me? What have I got to do with it?' Mackey protested.

'Kevin's your brother too. It's about time you learnt how to change a nappy, so you won't grow up like my dad.'

'No way! Get lost!'

'Then I won't let him be your brother any more.'

The others were laughing at the look on Mackey's face.

'She's right, Mackey. Go on!' Orla giggled.

'Get stuffed!'

'OK, gang — get him!' Orla signalled to the others and they dragged Mackey to his feet. They pulled him, wriggling and protesting, through Conker Woods and out into the lane. Joan was leading the way, with a determined look on her face.

When they reached Joan's gate, Mackey hissed furiously, 'Leggo of me! I can walk on my own. I never said I wasn't going to do it, did I?'

The gang let him go.

Mackey walked through the gateway after Joan with as much dignity as he could muster. The pair of them disappeared into Joan's kitchen, closing the door behind them. The rest of the gang sat on Joan's back grass to wait.

☆   ☆   ☆

It was a long time before Joan and Mackey returned. Joan, beaming, indicated that everything had gone according to plan.

'He didn't do it! I don't believe you!' Orla laughed.

'He did. He was really good, too. And Kevin stayed still for him — which is more than he does for me.'

'Well, it must have been a nice clean nappy, then,' said Jonathan.

Mackey was saying nothing. He had a smug look on his face.

'No, it wasn't!' Joan exclaimed. 'That's the point. It was messy. I showed Mackey how to clean Kevin up with baby-wipes. Then he put the new nappy on. My dad came in while he was doing it, and he was really impressed.'

They all stared at Mackey in amazement.

Mackey shrugged nonchalantly. 'Nothing to it. Anyone could do it!' And he glanced slyly at Jonathan and Muggins.

Jonathan, alarmed, quickly decided he wasn't staying around to see who was next for lessons. 'Race you to the Red Belly!' he yelled, running into Conker Woods with Muggins close on his heels.

Mackey, however, wasn't in a hurry anywhere.

He rummaged in his pockets and produced a cigarette butt and a box of matches. He lit the butt and, with his eyes closed and his head thrown back, inhaled deeply. He held his breath for a few seconds, then blew a huge and utterly perfect smoke-ring, which hovered over his head like a halo.

'Hey, look — Saint Mackey!' jeered Orla.

Felicity spluttered, trying not to laugh.

'Leave him alone,' Joan said.

But Mackey wasn't listening; he was basking in his new-found glory. The fellas in the pub weren't going to believe this one!

DISASTER STRIKES

Three days later, the gang were up the Red Belly, plane-spotting from its highest branches. Most of the gang were, anyway — Orla was sitting down at the foot of the tree, reading a Mills and Boon novel. She was totally absorbed in a most exciting part where the hero tried to have his wicked way with the ravishing purple-haired heroine ... or, rather, she was attempting to be totally absorbed. Columbus, in sheer frustration at not being able to climb the Red Belly with the rest of the gang, was trying to climb up Orla instead.

'Get down, Columbus. Get *down* .... Mackey, can't you control your dog? Mackey!'

There was little sympathy for her from above.

'Nothing to stop her coming up here,' Mackey declared belligerently. 'She's sitting in Columbus's place, anyway. What does she expect?'

'She spent nearly an hour doing her nails this morning,' Muggins said. 'Three coats and a top coat — my mum nearly went wild. That stuff doesn't half stink, too.' He pulled a face.

Felicity shook her head in bewilderment. 'I can't understand how anyone could consider nails important — I mean, more important than being able to do things like climbing trees.'

'My mum considers nails important,' Mackey observed, 'but it sure doesn't stop her doing things.' Mackey's mum always had long red nails.

'Talking about doing things, what are we going to do about Harold?' Jonathan asked.

'Nothing,' Mackey said.

'Why nothing?'

'Who wants the Captain's Table anyway? Harold can hear everything we say when he's up the Yellow Belly. He's got his half of the woods and we've got ours. Let's leave it at that.'

'He's not getting the Tunnel as well!' Jonathan protested. 'That's in his half.'

The Tunnel was one of their secret hiding-places. Formed by the arch of an old hedge leaning against the remains of a stone wall, it was overgrown with brambles and bushes, so nobody would know that it was there. The gang had found it entirely by accident. It had always been a handy bolt-hole when they were in trouble of any sort.

'Harold doesn't even know where the Tunnel is,' Felicity pointed out. 'We can still use it if we want to.'

'It's got too small for us all,' Joan said. 'It's really squashy now.'

'I like things squashy,' Muggins declared.

'Well, it's not secret any more, after last year,' Mackey said. 'My ma knows where it is, and so do the police.'

'You're not blaming us for telling!' Felicity exclaimed. 'We didn't have a choice. Joan's mum thought Kevin had been stolen by a desperate criminal.'

'He had!' Muggins smirked, and ducked as Mackey took a swipe at him. Mackey missed, so he started to rock his branch backwards and forwards, trying to bash it into Muggins's branch.

'Cut it out!' squealed Muggins. 'I nearly fell off that time.'

Mackey, satisfied, calmed down. 'Parents can be right dense,' he said. 'I was only showing the little fella all our secret places. The police made such a fuss! Why can't they go and bother proper criminals?'

'Finding Kevin was more important than telling about the Tunnel,' Felicity said defensively.

'Still ... it's not the same when it's not secret,' Mackey insisted.

'I know,' Felicity agreed sadly. She hadn't felt quite the same about it since then either.

A low rumbling filled the sky.

'There's a plane coming!' Mackey shouted, all else forgotten. It was coming in from behind them, hanging low in the sky.

'It must've been circling around, waiting to land,' Mackey said excitedly. 'It's coming in really slow.'

The rumble grew to a roar, and talk became impossible. The plane passed directly overhead, blotting out the sky. The wheels were down and it looked as if it were going to land just beyond Conker Road. The gang watched it pass over the houses and continue onwards at the same slow pace until, far off in the distance, it eased down to land at the airport.

'That was great!' Mackey crowed. 'A really good one!'

'I thought it was going to fall out of the sky before it reached the airport,' Muggins said.

'It was like a big spaceship going overhead,' said Jonathan. 'You know the way they always show them in films?'

'There's another one coming!' Muggins yelled.

They looked behind, but couldn't see anything. Then they realised that the noise was coming from in front of them — and it wasn't a plane, either.

'Look!' screeched Mackey. 'A JCB!'

The JCB was trundling down Conker Lane, past Jonathan and Felicity's house. It reached the corner and slowly turned to make its way along the back part of the lane.

'After it, quick!' Mackey shouted.

He slid down his branch and descended below the

canopy of Conker Woods, followed by the rest of the gang, racing one another to see who would be first into the Crow's Nest. From there they swung down the branches and tumbled to the ground in a series of rapid parachute rolls. Mackey had taught them all to do parachute rolls two summers ago; if they ever had to make an emergency leap out of a plane, he explained, it would be handy to know how to fall without hurting themselves. They landed at Orla's feet in an untidy heap. Columbus got so excited that he ran around in circles, barking ecstatically.

'What's going on?' demanded Orla in bewilderment.

'Come on and you'll see!' Jonathan shouted, as they all raced towards Conker Lane. Orla put her book in her pocket and followed.

The JCB was already parked at the end of the lane, almost blocking the Duggans' gate. The driver had left the cab and was standing in the laneway, talking to two other men. The gang recognised the grey-haired man and the young man with the ponytail — they were the ones who had demolished the haunted gate-lodge.

The gang stood and stared.

'What are they up to now?' Jonathan whispered.

'Let's find out,' said Mackey.

The gang sauntered along the lane until they were nearly level with the workmen.

'Hi again!' Mackey called cheerily.

The men nodded at them, and the young man smiled. Encouraged, Mackey continued, 'What are you doing here?'

'We're going to build a wall,' the grey-haired man said.

'A wall! Where?' Joan asked, astonished.

'Here.' The man gestured along the lane.

'You're going to build a wall in Conker Lane?'

'Along the edge of the woods,' the JCB driver explained.

'But ... hold on!' Felicity protested. 'If you build a wall, we won't be able to get into the woods.'

'Sorry!' The grey-haired man turned away and picked up some wooden stakes and string that he had left on the ground.

Mackey stepped forward belligerently. 'Hey! Just a minute! You can't build a wall here.'

'Yes we can, kiddo,' said the young man with the ponytail.

'No you can't! It's our woods!'

'It belongs to the County Council,' the young man pointed out gently, 'and now it's going to be part of the grounds of the new retirement home.'

'You mean ...' Mackey stuttered, outraged, 'you mean they're giving our woods away to a lot of *old* people?'

'That's just about it,' said the grey-haired man. 'Now, if you don't mind ... we've got work to do.'

He gestured to the gang to stand back out of the way. The ponytailed man was already busy cutting at some bushes that overhung the lane. The men set to work, measuring and staking out the area to be dug up for foundations. The gang watched in consternation.

There was a sound of trampling boots; then the big foreman they'd tangled with before came out of the woods.

He scowled when he saw them. 'Clear off outa here, you kids!' he shouted.

Felicity felt anger rising inside her like a tide. 'We won't clear off,' she shouted back. 'This is our lane. We live here.'

'You clear off yourselves,' yelled Mackey.

'You're not taking our woods!' Jonathan cried. 'We won't let you!'

Columbus decided to join in. He ran at the big foreman, growling. The foreman backed away.

'Get rid of that dog or I'll kick his teeth in,' he spat.

Mackey, knowing he could do just that, was alarmed. He called Columbus. 'Here, boy! Here!'

Columbus, as usual, ignored him. He was having too much fun. Mackey had to grab him by the collar and drag him away to the side of the lane, then hold on to the collar for dear life as Columbus struggled to free himself.

The foreman had gone to the bottom of the lane, to talk to the JCB driver. The other men were still measuring the ground. The gang watched them miserably, wondering what to do. The men ignored them completely.

After a while, tired of just standing there, the gang went and sat in Joan's back garden — way up at the top, so that they could talk in private. Mackey still kept a firm grip on Columbus.

'We have to stop them!' Felicity said passionately. 'We have to do *something*!'

'It'll have to be a quick something,' said Orla. 'That wall will be built in a day or two, and then it'll be too late.'

'We'll protest to the County Council ....' Mackey hissed. 'Hey! Stoppit, you pesky dog!' Columbus was doing his own protesting, and Mackey was getting tired of his dragging on the collar.

'A protest! That's it!' Felicity clapped her hands. 'We'll have a protest march.'

'Brilliant idea!' Orla agreed.

Mackey, still struggling with Columbus, nodded enthusiastically.

Jonathan, too, approved. 'That'll get every house on Conker Road involved.'

'People will be horrified when they hear what's happening,' Felicity said. 'They'll be sure to help us stop it, won't they?'

'Of course they will,' Muggins exclaimed. 'Aren't they always talking about protecting trees?'

Joan was frowning. 'But nobody's touching the trees. People mightn't care if the trees aren't being cut down.'

'That's not the point,' Felicity insisted. 'The woods are being taken away from the children of Conker Road — not just us, future generations too. There'll be no woods for your Kevin, or for Carly, or Shane, or Conor, or Aisling. They have to care about that ... don't they?'

'We'll soon find out,' Orla said.

The gang started making plans for the protest march. Jonathan slipped back to the Red Belly to fetch the logbook and, on his return, prepared to make a list.

'What's first?' he asked, pen poised over the paper.

'Cardboard boxes, for making placards,' Mackey said.

'Black marker pens,' Joan proposed. 'Big ones, so the writing will be good and clear.'

'What'll we say?'

'Conker Woods for the people of Conker Road,' offered Muggins.

Orla shook her head. 'Too long.'

'Save Conker Woods,' Felicity suggested.

'That's one, anyway,' agreed Jonathan, writing it down. 'Any more ideas?'

'County Council keep out!' Muggins offered.

'Out of where?' Orla protested. 'That's not a complete message.'

'Yes it is,' Felicity said. 'If we have a few placards saying "Save Conker Woods", then Muggins's message will be clear too.'

'It should be "Old folks keep out!",' Mackey said sourly.

'We can't say that! We'd never get anyone on our side,' Felicity pointed out. 'Our parents are old — how would they like that?'

'I meant people older than our folks.'

'So you're going to put an age on it?'

'Yeah,' Mackey replied. 'Everyone over sixty, keep out!'

'Sounds daft,' Muggins observed.

'It *is* daft,' Orla said impatiently.

'Be serious, Mackey!' Felicity entreated. 'We need ideas, proper ideas.'

'I have one of those, all right,' said Mackey, with a sudden gleam in his eye. 'What time is it?'

Orla looked at her watch. 'Half past twelve. Why?'

Mackey got up and signalled to them to follow. They trailed down the garden after him until they reached the back wall. Mackey was looking over the wall, into the lane.

'They've gone!' he chortled.

The lane was empty — except for the JCB parked by the Duggans' gate. A row of wooden pegs had been hammered into the ground, marking the line of the proposed new wall.

'They've only gone for lunch,' Jonathan said. 'They'll be back in an hour to start digging.'

'Well, I hope they bring their teaspoons!' Mackey laughed. 'Here, mind Columbus for me.'

He offered Columbus's collar to Jonathan, who took hold of it, while Columbus protested vigorously.

'Don't let him go, whatever happens. OK?' said Mackey.

'OK,' Jonathan promised, mystified.

Mackey strolled out into the lane. With his hands in his pockets, he casually approached the JCB. The next minute, he was up fiddling with the cab door, and in an instant he had it open. He got into the driver's seat and slammed the door shut.

The others stared, still not sure what Mackey was up to.

They soon found out.

With a great cough, the engine came to life. Then Mackey had the JCB turned around and was driving it along the lane. The gang ran out of Joan's garden as

Mackey rounded the corner expertly and went trundling up Conker Lane, towards the road.

The others raced after him. Jonathan was finding it difficult to hold Columbus, who was determined to catch up with Mackey. He could see why Mackey had made him promise not to let go.

They reached the top of the lane just as Mackey swung the JCB out onto the road. Mackey looked back and gave a cheeky wave. Then, with the JCB at full throttle now that the way was clear, he roared off down Conker Road.

Jonathan signalled frantically for the others to stop.

'Get down,' he hissed. 'Don't let anyone see you!'

They crouched by the Kellys' front garden wall and peeped cautiously around the corner. The JCB was almost at the bottom of the road. They watched, hardly able to believe what was happening, as it turned left and disappeared out of sight.

'What are you doing there?'

The sharp call came from behind and above them.

Mrs Finnerty was leaning out of her bedroom window, staring at them with deep suspicion.

'What are you doing?' she demanded again.

'Nothing, Mrs Finnerty,' Felicity answered.

'Why are you all sitting in the lane?'

'We like sitting in the lane,' Muggins answered.

'You're up to no good — I can see that a mile off,' Mrs Finnerty shouted. 'Go home, the lot of you!'

'Have a nice day yourself!' muttered Jonathan. He got up and dragged Columbus, with difficulty, back down the lane and through the side gate into his garden. The others reluctantly followed.

'Why did you stop us going after Mackey?' demanded Muggins, as soon as they could talk safely.

'Why do you think?' Jonathan asked. 'Chances are, nobody noticed he was driving. If we ran after him it would only attract attention; then everyone would see.'

'Good thinking,' said Orla.

'I'd have gone after him too,' Joan admitted.

'Well, that's what being a leader is all about,' Jonathan said importantly. 'Making split-second decisions about things.'

'Columbus is making a decision too!' Felicity started to giggle.

Jonathan had failed to notice Columbus cocking his leg. Too late, he felt the stream of warm liquid hit his calf and pour down into his shoe. Swearing loudly, he let Columbus go. Columbus took off at top speed, dashing out the gate and up the lane towards Conker Road.

'It's all right,' Orla said. 'He can't do any harm now.'

'Wonder where Mackey's gone?' Muggins was jittery with the excitement of it all.

'He turned in to the old estate,' said Joan. 'He'll probably ride around until he runs out of fuel.'

'He wouldn't be that stupid,' Orla said. 'Somebody would recognise him sooner or later.'

'Or report his driving,' Felicity laughed.

'Nothing wrong with his driving,' Jonathan said ruefully. He was sitting on the grass, removing his sodden shoe and sock. 'He drove that JCB like a professional.'

The gang were silent. After all this time, Mackey was still surprising them with his skills.

'We'd better lie low this afternoon,' said Jonathan. 'That foreman will be hopping mad. Meet you all in the Tunnel later. We can discuss tactics for tomorrow.'

'What about Mackey?' Joan asked.

'He'll find us,' Jonathan said. 'He always does. That dog of his is like a bloodhound.'

The Police Take an Interest

Mackey didn't turn up until three o'clock. By then, the others had been waiting for him for over an hour.

Columbus was first into the Tunnel, and he gave a delighted bark on seeing the rest of the gang already there.

'Shut up, silly dog,' Jonathan scolded. 'This place is meant to be secret.'

'Some secret, with the racket you're making,' Mackey said with a grin, hauling himself in after Columbus.

The Tunnel was a squash at the best of times, but with Columbus on the rampage it was ridiculous. He pushed his way up and down in great excitement, completely oblivious to the fact that he was climbing over arms and legs and shoulders and heads. Finally he settled down on top of Mackey, and, after giving him a huge lick on the face, fell asleep.

'He's tired,' Mackey said. 'We had a long walk — he followed me all the way into the old estate.'

'What did you do with the JCB?' Jonathan demanded, unable to contain his curiosity any longer.

Mackey grinned. 'I hid it in a tree-tent. The branches come right down to the ground, so it should take some finding. I'd an awful job getting it in there in the first place.'

The gang stared at Mackey, full of admiration.

'The workmen will be rightly mad,' Felicity said. 'I'd like to have seen their faces when they discovered it was missing.'

'Where did you learn to drive a JCB?' Muggins

asked, in total awe of Mackey's accomplishment.

'I learnt years ago.' Mackey shrugged casually. 'Fella in the pub taught me — he has a builder's yard. He lets me drive around his yard whenever I want.'

'You don't have a licence,' Joan said disapprovingly.

'Don't need one on private property,' Mackey shot back.

'You weren't on private property today.'

'That was different,' Mackey said. 'It was an emergency.'

'It was illegal.'

'So?'

'But you got into the JCB without any keys,' Muggins butted in, 'and started it, too .... How did you do that?'

Mackey shrugged again. 'Easy, once you know how. Fella in the pub showed me. He said it could come in handy in case of lost keys.'

'Wish I knew a fella in the pub,' Muggins said enviously.

'Let's get on with our campaign,' suggested Jonathan. 'They'll find the JCB sooner or later, but it gives us time to act.'

He opened the logbook and, with difficulty, managed to extract a Biro from his pocket.

'Now — we've got cardboard boxes, and marking pens, and ideas for two placards .... What else?'

'Sticks,' Felicity said, 'for holding up the placards.'

'Swords!' beamed Muggins.

'What?' the rest of the gang said together.

'Swords. Remember the wooden ones we made when we had our pirate play, *Blood and Guts on Treasure Island*? They're still in our shed. We could tie the placards to them, no bother.'

'Brilliant, Muggins!' Jonathan noted it down in the logbook. 'What else?'

'Who's going to march?' Joan asked. 'I mean, as well

as us. Are we going to ask Harold?'

'I'm not asking him, anyway,' said Mackey.

'Felicity will,' Jonathan decided.

'Thanks for consulting me!' Felicity retorted.

'You don't mind, Sis. You know you don't. And Harold likes you.'

'Oh ... all right. I'll talk to him.'

'Get him to bring Billy and Mark, too. We'll have the protest march at two o'clock tomorrow. That should give us plenty of time to get ready. Everyone agreed?'

They all nodded.

'What about Carly and Shane?' Felicity asked Orla. 'Would your mum let them march?'

Orla looked surprised but said, 'I don't see why not. I'll ask her. Carly would be thrilled.'

'And I could bring Kevin in his buggy,' Joan put in. 'He should be there too. After all, it's his future that's at stake.'

'Great!' Felicity exclaimed. 'And maybe some of the people on Conker Road will join in, once they see us marching.'

The whole thing sounded very satisfactory.

Orla looked at her watch and said, 'It's well after four. Those men should be gone.'

Jonathan snapped the logbook shut. 'Right, then, let's get out of here. I can hardly breathe! Race you to the top of the Red Belly!'

☆   ☆   ☆

That evening, Mackey and his mum were just finishing their tea when there was a knock at the front door. Mrs McCarthy went to answer it.

She was back in a couple of minutes.

'Ignatius, there's a policeman here. What have you been up to now?'

'Nothing,' Mackey said quickly.

'Well, he wants to see you. He won't tell me what's going on.'

Mackey got up from the table, taking a big slice of bread and butter with him. He followed his mother to the sitting-room.

The policeman was all too familiar. Mackey had come face to face with him in the Tunnel last year, when the police had been looking for Kevin.

'Hi, there!' said the policeman, trying to be friendly.

Mackey stared at him, stony-faced.

'What's this all about?' Mrs McCarthy demanded sharply.

'A JCB went missing from the lane behind your house today,' the policeman explained. 'I thought young Ignatius here might be able to help us with our enquiries.'

'Why me?' Mackey asked belligerently.

'Well, the JCB was stolen between half past twelve and half past one. The workmen said you kids were hanging around the lane.'

'We were in our gardens, minding our own business,' Mackey said.

'Did you see anyone else?'

'We saw the workmen.'

'Besides the workmen?'

'No.'

'Did you see the JCB being driven away?'

'No,' said Mackey truthfully.

'You must have heard it!'

'Yeah ... I heard it.'

'Do you know who was driving it?'

'Was it the JCB driver?'

'Hardly,' the policeman said in exasperation, 'if it was being stolen.'

'Do I get three guesses?' Mackey asked innocently.

But Mrs McCarthy had had enough. 'Really, Guard,

I don't see where all this is leading.'

'I just feel Ignatius might be able to tell us something,' the policeman said carefully, staring hard at Mackey.

'Don't look at me like that!' Mackey protested. 'You'd think I stole the stupid JCB, the way you're going on. I'm too young even to have a driving licence.'

Mrs McCarthy glared at the policeman, who said quickly, 'It's not just you. We're making enquiries at every house on Conker Road.'

'I'm glad to hear it,' Mrs McCarthy said icily.

There was a strained silence.

Mackey started to chomp on his slice of bread and butter.

Finally the policeman said, 'Well ... I won't take up any more of your time.'

Mrs McCarthy showed him out, closing the door firmly behind him.

'You'll end up in jail one of these days,' Joan warned Mackey, the next morning. They were all sitting in the Kellys' garden, making the placards for the protest march.

'I've been already,' Mackey retorted.

'That was only for a few hours ... and it wasn't really being in jail properly.'

'They only lock bad people away,' Mackey said firmly, 'and I'm not bad ... am I?'

Joan sighed. 'No, Mackey, you're not. But you'd better watch yourself all the same.'

'Well, it's not as if I *stole* the JCB,' Mackey said. 'I only hid it. They'll find it sooner or later.'

'That's just as bad. It's a crime too.'

'No it's not,' Mackey insisted. 'It's a legitimate protest. Those women who camped on Greenham Common for years did things like that. Fella in the pub told me.'

'Why did women camp on a common for years?' Muggins asked.

'They were protesting about missiles that were being stored at a military base there. They had a peaceful protest, but they used to tear down fences all the same, and have sit-ins on roofs and things. Ours is a peaceful protest too. I just hid the JCB so we could protest before they built the wall.'

'I suppose ... when you put it like that ....' Joan was looking confused now.

'Mackey's right,' Felicity said. 'It gives us a chance

of stopping things before they start.'

'Did you see the *speed* of Mackey, bombing down Conker Road?' gloated Jonathan. 'I wish I'd had a video camera!'

'That would be evidence, silly,' Orla said. 'As it is, there's none. No one seems to have seen Mackey at the wheel.'

'Maybe someone did, but wasn't sure,' Mackey said. 'That policeman was awfully suspicious. I think he knew something.'

'They can't prove anything,' Jonathan said.

Muggins wasn't listening. He was too busy with his placard, which he'd tied to the handle of one of the swords. He held it up.

'Is this all right?'

The placard read, 'County Council Keep Out'.

'It looks great, Muggins,' Felicity said. 'Let's get the others finished.'

Orla was making a long banner for Carly and Shane out of an old sheet of wallpaper. 'Keep Conker Woods For Us,' it said, in big green letters.

Felicity and Mackey and Joan started tying their placards to the other swords. They all said the same thing — 'Save Conker Woods' — but Felicity said this didn't matter. 'We need to get the message across as many times as possible.'

'Have you seen Harold?' Orla enquired.

'No. I couldn't find him yesterday, and he hasn't gone by yet today,' Felicity said. 'I've been watching out for him.'

It was another ten minutes before Harold appeared. As he passed by with Arnie, Felicity jumped up and went after him. He was halfway down the lane before she got to the gate.

'Harold!' she called. 'Can we talk to you?'

Harold stopped and turned around. 'About what?'

'Come in and we'll tell you.'

Harold hesitated for a moment. 'Is Columbus there?'

Felicity nodded.

Harold patted Arnie on the head. 'Sit!' he commanded.
Arnie sat.

'Good boy!' Harold said. 'Now stay!' He backed
away from Arnie, repeating 'Stay!', and when he
reached the gate he said 'Stay!' once more. Arnie
stayed, but he watched Harold with mournful eyes as
he went through the gate with Felicity.

Harold stood in the Kellys' garden and looked at the
notices with astonishment. 'What are you doing?' he
asked.

'What does it look like?' Felicity said. 'We're having
a protest march.'

'About what exactly?'

'The Council's taking Conker Woods. Haven't you
heard?'

'They're not taking it all. Only half of it.'

Felicity stared at him. 'Who told you that?'

'The foreman told me. I asked. They're taking the
bottom half of the woods to be the grounds for a Senior
Citizens' Retirement Home.'

'But that's our half!' Felicity cried. 'That's the Red
Belly and all our climbing trees!'

'I know.' Harold looked uncomfortable.

'Don't you *care*?' Felicity wailed.

'Well ... I'll still have my half.'

'Oh no you won't!' Jonathan snapped. 'They're
going to build a wall right along the lane. You won't
even be able to get into the woods.'

'Yes I will,' Harold replied. 'They're leaving a gap at
the Finnertys' end, for access. They explained it all to me.'

The gang were speechless.

Finally Felicity said, 'Are they building another wall
through the woods, then — to join up with the field?'

Harold nodded.

'So they'll have to cut down trees?'

'No,' Harold said.

'How else can they build a wall through the woods? They'll have to get a JCB through.'

'They must be doing it by hand or something. Nobody said anything to me about cutting down trees.'

Felicity frantically tried to rescue the situation. 'Well, we're protesting anyway,' she said firmly. 'They've no business taking even half of the woods away. It belongs to the children of Conker Road. Will you and Billy and Mark join our protest march?'

'Billy and Mark aren't here.'

'You can ring them.'

'They're out this morning,' Harold stated flatly.

'Well, bring them along this afternoon, then. We aren't protesting until two o'clock.'

'I'd have to ask them first,' Harold said. 'I couldn't make a promise like that without consulting them.'

'Rubbish!' Mackey scoffed. 'They'll do whatever you tell them. Sure, they follow you around like sheep.'

'I'd have to consult them,' Harold insisted doggedly.

Felicity resorted to pleading. 'We'd really like you along, Harold ... and we need the extra numbers.'

But Harold was still being evasive. 'I'll ask my gang when I see them. Is there anything else?'

Felicity shook her head.

Harold left the garden and disappeared back down the lane.

'Great help he was,' Jonathan sniffed.

'Well, at least I tried,' Felicity said defensively. 'Do you believe what he said?'

'About what?'

'About the Council taking just our half of the woods?'

'It's probably true,' Orla said. 'Harold has a way of getting these things right.'

'But they can't!' Felicity wailed. 'They can't take the Red Belly away from us and leave Harold with the Yellow Belly. It's not fair! The Red Belly is ours! They can't hand it over to a lot of old people. They just *can't*!'

'They can,' said Joan sadly. 'They can do what they like.'

'Well, they'll have a fight on their hands,' Felicity vowed. 'They're not getting the woods. They're not! We'll protest and protest until they change their minds.' She picked up one of the swords and angrily drove it, point down, into the ground.

'Great stuff!' said Mackey approvingly. He cupped his hands around his mouth and roared, 'Up the Red Belly!'

'Let's finish these placards, then,' Orla said. 'We haven't a lot of time left.'

The gang went back to work with renewed fervour.

By two o'clock, the gang were all assembled at the top
of Conker Lane, ready to march. There was no sign of
Harold, but Carly and Conor had come, and Joan had
brought Kevin in his buggy. They agreed to spread out
as much as possible, so that the protest would look a
bit bigger.

Felicity and Mackey were to lead, each carrying a
'Save Conker Woods' placard. Felicity's lettering was
done in green. Mackey's lettering was in a double
thickness of black, and he had drawn a border of skulls
and crossbones around the edges of the placard.

'That's brilliant, Mackey!' Felicity exclaimed. 'It
looks exactly the way I feel. I don't know why I didn't
do mine the same.'

'One is enough,' Mackey grinned. 'Mine is unique!'

Joan came next, with Kevin in the buggy. She had
tied her placard to her chest to leave her hands free.
Carly and Conor were behind her, each proudly
clutching a corner of their 'Keep Conker Woods For Us'
banner. Orla had done the letters, but the two children
had painted little trees in all the empty spaces.

Orla stood behind, keeping an eye on them. She had
cut her own placard into the shape of a tree and
painted it green. The white letters led downwards:

Save

Conker

Woods

Jonathan and Muggins brought up the rear. Not only
did they have placards to hold up, they also had extra

ones pinned onto their backs. This was Felicity's idea — 'so people behind us will know what the protest is about too.'

Mackey waved his skulls and crossbones in the air. 'Ready to march, gang?'

'Yes!'

'Off we go, then.'

They moved forward to the edge of Conker Road. Mackey stopped.

'Which way?' he asked Felicity. The lane was exactly halfway down the road.

'Up,' said Felicity. 'Then we'll have a good run down again, all the way to the bottom.'

The protest march turned out onto Conker Road. Felicity set up the chant: 'Save Conker Woods! Save Conker Woods!'

Carly and Conor were thrilled. They screamed the words out, and even Kevin tried to join in, crying 'Da-da-da-da!' and waving his arms and legs in great excitement.

A few people came to their windows as the protest march passed by, but none of them came out to their gardens. Felicity made a beckoning sign to one woman who was peeping out through her net curtains; the woman disappeared immediately, and that was the last they saw of her.

'You'd think they would come out and support us,' Felicity fumed.

'Maybe it'll be better on the way down,' Mackey said. 'They know we're here now.'

They reached the top of Conker Road, where it joined up with the big main road that led to the city. There was a bit of confusion here, as they all tried to turn around together and kept bumping into one another. But finally they sorted themselves out and were ready to go again. The full length of Conker Road stretched ahead of them.

'Save Conker Woods!' yelled Mackey. 'Save Conker Woods!'

'Save Conker Woods!' screamed the others, as they set off back down the road.

This time, there were a few people watching from doorways. Mrs Finnerty was standing on old Fitzy's doorstep with her apron on. Mackey's mum was out in the garden; so was Felicity and Jonathan's mum. Orla and Muggins's mum was at the gate with Shane and Aisling, who were waving energetically.

'This is more like it,' Felicity said with satisfaction.

But beyond the Duggans' house there were few people paying any attention at all. One or two came out briefly, to see what all the noise was about, then went inside again.

The gang did their best, waving their placards and shouting at the tops of their lungs, 'Save Conker Woods! Save Conker Woods!' At the bottom of Conker Road they turned, a bit less chaotically this time, and started to march back up again.

Carly and Conor were getting tired. Unable to keep exactly the same distance apart, they had managed to split their banner in half, and were trying to hold up a portion each. This didn't make the message any easier to read. Kevin had fallen asleep.

When they reached Conker Lane again, Harold was standing there, hands in his pockets.

'You're wasting your time,' he called.

'We are not!' Felicity shouted back furiously.

'Where's the press?'

'What press?' Felicity demanded.

'Exactly,' Harold said.

'What are you talking about, you little squirt?' Mackey roared.

Harold looked at them calmly. 'There's not much use in having a protest march if you haven't notified the papers,' he pointed out. 'Who'll know about it if there are no reporters here?'

'The people of Conker Road will know about it,' Felicity retorted.

Harold looked up and down the road. 'Don't see too many of them out.'

'You're a great help, you are,' snapped Mackey. 'Why don't you come and do your bit?'

'You said you'd ask Billy and Mark,' Felicity reminded him.

'I can't ask them if they're not here, can I?'

'You could join us yourself.'

'I have to consult with my gang.'

'He's like a bloody parrot,' said Mackey in disgust. 'Come on! Who needs him anyway?'

They set off up Conker Road again. 'Save Conker Woods!' they shouted. 'Save Conker Woods!'

By the time they had marched to the top of the road, then back down to the bottom, then back up again, they were all getting tired. Orla was carrying Conor, and Carly was gamely trying to hold on to both sections of the banner by herself.

When they reached the top of the road for the third time, there wasn't a soul to be seen apart from themselves. Even Harold had disappeared.

Joan sat down on the kerb. 'It's no use,' she wailed. 'Harold's right.'

'He's not right,' Felicity replied angrily. 'We can make people notice. We can knock on doors and ask for people's support. We'll ask them to tell other people. We can get them to sign a petition.'

The entire protest march had now collapsed onto the pavement. Only Felicity was left standing.

'Come on!' she insisted. 'Get up! We've got to keep going!'

'You start, Sis,' said Jonathan wearily. 'You're good

at that sort of thing.'

'We're just getting our breaths back,' panted Muggins.

'I have my hands full with Carly and Conor,' Orla said. Conor had fallen asleep in her arms and Carly was leaning against her, exhausted.

'And I'm minding Kevin,' said Joan.

'Well, I'll do it myself, then!' Felicity flounced off to knock on the nearest door.

A woman answered.

'Will you give your support to save Conker Woods?' Felicity asked.

'From what?' The woman looked surprised.

'The Council are taking the woods to be the grounds for an Old People's Home.'

'The whole woods?'

'Well, no,' Felicity answered. 'Only half, but —'

'Haven't you got the other half, then?'

'Yes ... but you don't understand ....'

The woman stepped forward onto the doorstep and looked at Felicity sharply. 'Are they cutting down trees?' she demanded.

'No ....'

'Well, then, what's the fuss about?'

'They're taking the half of the woods that we play in. We have this marvellous tree —'

The woman cut her short. 'You'll just have to play in the other half, so, won't you?'

'But it's not fair!' Felicity desperately tried to gather her thoughts into an argument. 'Everyone can use the woods at the moment. It ... it's a ... a local amenity.' She felt a surge of pride at remembering the phrase. 'But now half of it is being handed over to old people.'

The woman drew herself up to her full height, folded her arms and glared at Felicity. 'Old people are entitled to things too. You think you kids are the only ones who can appreciate a woods?'

'No — I never said that ....'

'I'm glad to hear it. Now, if you'll excuse me ....' The woman went back in and shut the door, leaving Felicity fuming on the doorstep.

Felicity went back to the others and sat down on the kerb.

'What did she say?' Mackey demanded.

'She didn't care,' Felicity seethed. 'She said that old people were entitled to things too.'

'What'll we do, then?' Jonathan was frowning.

'Think of something else,' said Mackey.

'Like what?' Muggins asked.

'Maybe we should just give up,' said Joan. 'They'll win anyway.'

Felicity got mad. 'We're *not* giving up! No way! Like Mackey says, we'll just think of something else.' But, to tell the truth, she felt a lot less sure than she sounded.

It was not going to be easy.

The next morning, the gang were back at old Fitzy's again. They were glad of something to do to keep their minds off the problem of Conker Woods.

'Saw your protest march yesterday,' Mrs Finnerty said as she let them in. 'Don't do much good, those things.'

'So we found out,' muttered Mackey.

'They do sometimes,' Felicity protested. 'We just didn't go about it the right way. We're not giving up, Mrs Finnerty — will you support us?'

'Oh, leave me out of it,' Mrs Finnerty said quickly. 'I have enough to be doing .... Off out into the garden with you, now.' She shooed them up the hall and through the kitchen, then doubled back and hurried upstairs before they could argue.

Mr Fitzhenry was pottering about, examining his flowerbeds.

'Hi, Mr Fitzhenry!' the gang chorused.

Mr Fitzhenry nodded to them and watched as Joan put a blanket down on the concrete for Kevin. Tiggy was sunning herself close by, but Scut took off down the garden with Columbus, in great glee, to play tag among the gooseberry bushes.

Mr Fitzhenry moved up to his seat by the kitchen door, where he could watch Kevin and keep him away from the shores while Joan did a bit of work.

Orla bagged the lawnmower, which was the thing least likely to damage her nails. She started to mow. Jonathan had decided to clip the edges of the lawn. The others got out trowels and hand-forks and set to weeding. Mackey took the hoe down to the fruit garden to weed around the gooseberry bushes. There, he could keep an eye on Columbus and be away from old Fitzy's eagle eye.

Mrs Finnerty brought them lemonade and biscuits at half past ten and they took a long and leisurely break, lying on the newly mown grass. Old Fitzy was drinking a mug of tea with one hand and holding a bottle of orange juice to Kevin's mouth with the other. Kevin was back in his buggy; he had fallen asleep, but every now and then he'd take a big suck on the bottle. Felicity had put out water for the dogs, and they drank thirstily before flopping down in the shade for a nap.

The garden was warm and quiet. The smell of grass was like perfume in the air.

'Bees sound really loud when you listen, don't they?' Mackey observed. He was lying with his head close to a fuchsia bush; a big bumblebee was busily going from bell to bell, gathering nectar.

'Bzzz,' Mackey droned in imitation. 'Bzzzzz ....'

There was a loud rumbling in the air. The sound got louder and louder. For a moment the gang were thoroughly confused.

Mackey was the first to cotton on. 'It's the JCB,' he reckoned.

They listened intently. The sound was coming from the direction of the lane.

Mackey took off down the garden. Using the rain-water barrel as a jump-off point, he vaulted over the wall into the woods.

He was back in a few minutes.

'It's the JCB, all right. Wonder how they found it?'

'Pity,' Jonathan said. 'I thought it would take them longer.'

'Two days isn't bad, though.' Mackey seemed pleased enough.

'Are they digging?' Felicity asked.

Mackey nodded. 'About to start, by the looks of it.'

'Think, everybody! We've got to stop them.'

'Let's finish the garden,' Orla suggested. 'We can think while we're doing it.'

They went back to work.

Orla discovered a blister on the palm of her hand and quickly passed the mower over to Jonathan. She sat on the back step, watching him mow, while she nursed her hand. Mr Fitzhenry had fallen asleep and was snoring loudly. Kevin was still asleep; his bottle had fallen to the ground. Orla picked it up and brought it in to Mrs Finnerty, who tut-tutted and declared that it needed a good scalding.

By a quarter past twelve, the garden was finished and the tools were stored away in the shed. The JCB had fallen silent. The gang made their departure, plans of action fermenting in their minds.

'Let's see what they've done,' Mackey said as they raced down the laneway.

There was no sign of the JCB, but a newly dug trench ran the length of Conker Lane. All the loose soil had been piled up along the edge of the woods.

'They're fierce cute,' Mackey observed. 'They've gone to lunch and taken the JCB with them.'

'I wonder why!' laughed Felicity.

'Well, they're in for a nasty surprise all the same.'

'What surprise?' asked Joan, who had just returned from leaving Kevin with her dad.

'When they get back from lunch, this trench will be nicely filled in again.'

'Who's going to fill it in?' Muggins asked, still not understanding.

'We are, daftie!'

'Hey, that's brilliant, that is. Just brilliant!' Jonathan gave Mackey a thump of approval.

'I hope you don't expect me to scoop soil with my fingers,' Orla said.

'Course not,' Mackey declared. 'That'd be too slow anyway. We need shovels, spades — anything — and quickly. We haven't much time.'

The gang scattered.

In minutes they were back, with whatever they could find that might be useful. Jonathan and Felicity had two big spades and a sizeable coal-shovel. Orla and Muggins had spades and shovels too. Joan said her garden spade was too big; she had brought along a couple of hand-trowels instead. Mackey had a rake.

Jonathan nearly fell into the trench with laughter when he saw Mackey's rake.

'What are you doing with that thing? It'll be like trying to catch water in a sieve!'

'No it won't,' Mackey said. 'Watch!'

He proceeded to demonstrate by standing on the lane side of the trench and raking a load of earth forward into the hole. He was greatly helped by the fact that a lot of the dug-up earth was in huge clods. The rake proved to be best of all for these.

'Come on!' Mackey urged the others. 'Get moving, gang!'

They set to with a will.

It was hard work. Columbus had to be removed to Mackey's garden and tied up, as he turned out to be such a nuisance — he was jumping back and forward along the trench until he was in danger of being hit by a shovel.

Within fifteen minutes, they were all red-faced and streaming with sweat.

'I thought doing old Fitzy's garden was hard,' Muggins complained. 'Compared to this, it's a doddle.'

'We'll never get it all filled in in time,' Joan panted. 'It's useless.'

'We don't have to get every inch done,' Mackey wheezed — he was out of breath too. 'If we get the middle properly filled in first, and work outwards, then it won't matter too much if little bits are left at each end.'

'Just as well we're in training,' Jonathan said. 'Doing old Fitzy's garden has made us fit.'

They dug and dug, and scraped and raked, and dug and dug .... Muggins disappeared at one point and came back wearing his wellington boots, having decided that it would be easiest to kick the soil back into the trench. He sat by the edge of the woods and used his feet as a bulldozer to push the earth forward.

'Hey, Muggins, that's a deadly idea!' Mackey said approvingly.

Muggins was making such good progress that Felicity abandoned her spade and did the same. The light coal-shovel that she'd brought along had broken in two, and she was finding the spade too heavy. Besides, her arms were aching unbearably. She sat beside Muggins, and together they pushed huge piles of earth back into the trench. Within minutes, Felicity's trainers were caked with soil.

'Mum'll love you when she sees those!' Jonathan called, from further along the lane.

'Your own aren't in such good nick,' Felicity retorted. 'Anyway, they'll wash.'

Everyone was filthy by now, but they didn't care. Time was racing along and they worked as fast as they could, which left them very little breath for talking. Shovel, shovel ... rake, rake ... shovel, shovel ... push, push ....

'Hurry! Hurry!' Mackey urged them. 'We've only got ten minutes left.'

They were hot and sticky and tired, and gasping for breath as if they'd been running for miles. But they put one last superhuman effort into the job. Shovel, shovel, scrape-scrape-scrape, shovel, shovel, shovel ....

Finally they collapsed across the trench, completely exhausted and unable to move another particle of earth.

'That's it,' Mackey said. 'We've done enough.'

The earth was slightly banked up in the trench now, so it made a nice hillock for sitting on. They sprawled out, trying to catch their breaths.

After a while, Jonathan started to chuckle. 'Wait till they see what we've done!'

'The foreman will be mad!' Muggins said. 'He'll kill us!'

'They're due back any minute,' Orla warned. 'We'd better scarper.'

Joan was sitting up, eyeing the filled-in trench and feeling suddenly deflated. 'Won't they just dig it all up again?' she said wearily. 'With the JCB, they'll have it done in no time.'

Mackey grinned. 'No they won't,' he said. 'Because we'll still be here!'

'What!'

The others sat up. Mackey was lounging comfortably on the pile of earth, with his hands behind his head.

'What are you on about?' Joan demanded.

Mackey delivered his trump card. 'We're having a sit-in,' he declared.

'A sit-in!' Muggins exclaimed in great excitement. 'I've never been on a sit-in before. What do we do?'

'We sit,' Mackey said. 'Right here. They can't use the JCB if we're still sitting on the trench.'

'The men will just pull us off,' Jonathan scoffed.

'No they won't,' Mackey told him. 'That's illegal. If they lay a hand on us, they're in big trouble.'

'How can you be sure?' Joan asked apprehensively.

'Fella in the pub told me.'

'Well, I just hope you're right.' Joan didn't look convinced.

'We'll find out quick enough,' Felicity whispered urgently. 'Here they come!'

The workmen had appeared at the bottom of the lane. They stopped and stared in astonishment at the filled-in trench. Then they spotted the gang.

The foreman's face went purple with rage. He clenched his fists and his teeth, and great sinews stood out on his neck. He let out a bellowing roar.

'Clear off outa there, you kids! Shift!'

Even though they were expecting it, they all jumped. Felicity's heart thumped in panic. Jonathan's mouth went dry, and Joan and Muggins were frozen to the spot. Orla, suddenly feeling unsteady, put out a hand for support and broke three fingernails on the edge of Jonathan's shovel.

Only Mackey stayed ice-cool.

'Can't you say anything else?' he enquired cheekily. 'We've heard that before. You're like a parrot!'

The foreman swore loudly and charged. He came at Mackey like a great, black, hissing steam-engine.

'Don't you lay a finger on me!' Mackey screamed. 'I'll have you up for assault of a minor!'

The other workmen rushed forward and grabbed the foreman, frantically trying to stop him.

'For God's sake, John, stop! Stop!' cried the grey-haired man. 'You can't touch him. He's only a child.'

The foreman stopped, hands still clenched, breathing heavily. He was inches away from Mackey, who hadn't moved.

The others *had* moved — well out of the firing-line. Jonathan and Joan had crawled one way along the trench, Felicity and Orla the other. Muggins was lying face down on the pile of earth with his hands over his head, sobbing in terror.

'Look what you did now,' Mackey scolded the fore-man. 'You've upset my friends!'

The foreman took several heaving breaths. Then he shrugged off the other men and visibly worked at calming himself down.

Finally he attempted an ingratiating smile.

'Be reasonable, sonny,' he said. 'We have a job to do. Fun's over. Now just get off that trench and go home.'

'I don't like people calling me "sonny",' Mackey said dangerously.

The foreman took another deep breath. 'Right. Let's do this your way. What's your name, then?'

'I don't give my name to strangers.'

'Now look here —'

They were suddenly interrupted by a loud rumbling sound. Something was driving down Conker Lane. The gang, presuming that it was the JCB, were greatly surprised to see a lorry turn the corner and come to a stop. It was a ready-mix concrete lorry.

The foreman sighed. He went over to talk to the lorry driver, and the gang could see them arguing. The driver was shaking his head. Finally the lorry started to back up Conker Lane, the way it had come.

The foreman was not pleased. He had a look of grim determination on his face. He approached the gang again.

'Happy now?' He cocked a thumb over his shoulder. 'That concrete should have been poured into this trench.' He pointed to where the gang were sitting.

No one answered. They were astonished that their plan was going so well.

'Now look here, kids,' the foreman started again, 'you've made your point. Will you please go home and let us get on with our work?'

'We're staying,' Mackey said.

'We'll see about that!' The foreman turned, beckoning to the other two men, and went in through Joan's back gate. They marched up the garden and knocked on Joan's back door. Jonathan stood up on the pile of earth to report their progress.

'Hey, can I come out and play?' The voice floated down from the end of the lane. Carly was hanging over the Duggans' gate, watching them with interest.

'No, you can't, Carly. You're not allowed out of the garden,' Orla replied shortly.

Carly's lip went down in a pout. She stared at Orla defiantly, then said, 'I'm telling on you .... You never came home for dinner, and Mammy's mad!' With that, she got down off the gate, and they could hear her shouting, 'Mammy! Mammy!'

'That's done it!' Orla muttered.

'Maybe she'll bring our dinner out to us,' Muggins said brightly. 'I'm starving.'

So were the rest of them.

'What are we going to do for food?' Joan asked.

'Just wait,' Mackey said. 'Some things are more important than eating.'

'Action stations, gang!' Jonathan warned, sitting down quickly. 'They're coming back.'

The workmen came up the garden and out into the lane again. Mr O'Brien was with them, carrying Kevin. He took in the scene with some astonishment.

'Joan, love, what's going on here?'

'We're having a sit-in, Dad,' Joan answered. 'Nobody gave us support on our protest march, so we're going to stop the wall being built by ourselves.'

'Oh ... I see.' He didn't seem to object.

At that moment Mrs Duggan came out through her garden gate, somewhat flustered. She shut the gate firmly behind her before Carly and Shane could get out. Carly started to whinge.

'What on earth are you doing?' Mrs Duggan asked the gang.

'We're having a sit-in, Mrs Duggan,' Joan explained, 'to stop the wall being built.'

The foreman was watching Mrs Duggan with a sly expression. 'Those kids will catch their deaths of cold, sitting on the damp earth,' he said.

Mrs Duggan got all worried. She examined the trench closely. The dug-up soil did, indeed, look damp.

'The man is right,' she said. 'And you've only got light clothes on.'

'Bring us our sleeping-bags, then, Mrs Duggan,' Mackey suggested. 'We can sit on them instead. We'll need them for tonight, anyway.'

'Tonight!' Mrs Duggan looked alarmed.

So did the rest of the gang.

'Tonight?' Joan said faintly.

'*Tonight*?' screeched Muggins. 'Are we sleeping here tonight?'

'We are,' Mackey said firmly. 'Tonight, and tomorrow night, and the night after that. To build that wall, they'll have to move us ... and *we — ain't — moving!*'

The workmen were exchanging worried glances. The foreman lost his temper. He rounded on the adults.

'Shift those bloody kids!' he roared.

Joan's dad bridled at his tone.

'Hold on a minute,' he said. 'The way I see it, they have a democratic right to protest.'

'They're obstructing the County Council!'

'The County Council are obstructing us!' Mackey shouted.

'The kids have a point,' Mr O'Brien informed the foreman. 'You're taking their woods.'

'We're taking half of the woods.'

'Well, you're taking it away from them, anyway.'

'Thanks, Dad!' Joan called.

'We have the law on our side,' the foreman threatened. 'It's too late for objecting. Planning permission was obtained last year. Nobody protested then.'

'We didn't know about it!' Mackey said.

'That's no excuse. It's too late now.'

'It's never too late,' Mackey declared. 'We're staying here for as long as it takes.'

There was a loud wail from the Duggans' garden. 'I'd better get back,' Mrs Duggan said. She hurried down the lane and through her back gate.

Mr O'Brien was admonishing the workmen. 'You're not to touch these kids,' he warned. 'Don't lay as much as a finger on them, or you'll have me to reckon with.'

'They'll soon get fed up.' The foreman shrugged. 'We can wait. Come on, men!' He turned and went into the woods. The other two men followed.

'Well, you've certainly upset them,' said Mr O'Brien.

'Good,' Mackey said. 'They've upset us and all.'

'I'm starving,' Muggins whined. 'Why didn't Mammy bring us our dinners?'

'Stop moaning, Muggins,' said Joan.

Mr O'Brien looked at the tired and dirty lot before him — tired, dirty, but determined.

'I suppose I'd better make a few sandwiches,' he said.

'Dad, you're brilliant!' Joan could hardly believe he was offering.

'Here. Look after Kevin while I do them.' Mr O'Brien dumped the child in Joan's lap.

'I knew there had to be a catch,' muttered Joan, as her dad disappeared down the garden path. 'Hey, keep still, Kevin. You have to stay here with us.' She locked her arms around the wriggling child.

'I hope he doesn't forget about the sandwiches,' Muggins said.

'Anything's possible.' Joan sounded resigned.

Kevin was investigating the pile of earth with interest. He closed his fist over a handful of clay and brought it to his mouth.

'Stop, Kevin. Stop!' Joan pulled his hand away and prised his fist open. Ignoring his protests, she cleaned away the earth. 'Dirty! Dirty!' she scolded.

Kevin started to bawl.

'Give the little fella to me,' said Mackey.

Joan passed Kevin over. Mackey sat him on his knee and started to jog him up and down. 'Ride a cock-horse to Banbury Cross ....' Kevin stopped crying and started chuckling instead.

'See? I knew I could make him stop,' said Mackey, pleased.

'So *this* is what you're up to?' The voice came from Mackey's back garden. Mrs McCarthy was standing under the cherry tree by the back wall, cigarette in hand. Mrs Kelly was beside her.

'We're having a sit-in, Mum!' Felicity called.

'I know,' Mrs Kelly said. 'Orla's mother phoned. I was just in the door from work.'

Mrs McCarthy took a long pull on her cigarette, then exhaled, blowing a cloud of smoke onto the air. 'How long are you planning to sit there?' she asked with amusement.

'As long as it takes,' Mackey replied.

'You might be in for quite a wait.'

'We don't care.'

Mrs McCarthy raised her eyebrows and laughed, saying something to Mrs Kelly which the gang couldn't hear. Mrs Kelly nodded.

'Well, have fun, then!' Mrs McCarthy said. 'See you later!' With a breezy wave of her hand, she took off up the garden.

'Ma! Ma! Wait ....' Mackey was outraged. 'She didn't even ask if we wanted anything!'

'Tea or lemonade?' Mrs Kelly was laughing too.

'My dad's making sandwiches,' Joan said.

'Oh? You don't need any sausage rolls, then.'

'Yes we do, Mum,' Felicity declared quickly.

'And make it lemonade,' Jonathan called.

'Lemonade what?'

'Fizzy,' said Muggins, licking his lips. The others burst into giggles. Mrs Kelly turned to go.

'Lemonade, *please*,' Jonathan shouted quickly. Mrs Kelly nodded, and went off up the garden after Mackey's mum.

It was just as well they'd expressed an interest in the sausage rolls. By the time they arrived, there was still no sign of Joan's dad with the sandwiches.

'He's a bit slow with things like that,' Joan defended him.

While Mrs Kelly doled out lemonade from a bottle into plastic beakers, Mrs McCarthy presented each of the gang with a thick paper napkin filled with hot sausage rolls.

'Everybody OK now?' Mrs McCarthy surveyed them, hands on hips.

The gang nodded, mouths crammed so full that they couldn't answer.

'We'll be back at the house. If you need us, just shout.'

The two women left, and the gang were on their own again.

Mackey fed Kevin some sausage roll, blowing on it to make sure it was cool enough, and gave him lemonade to drink. Kevin was perfectly happy.

They'd all eaten their fill and were feeling stuffed when Joan's dad appeared with a plateful of cheese sandwiches.

'Where have you *been*?' Joan scolded. 'It's over an hour since you offered to make them.'

'Sorry, pet, but I had to wait for the bread to defrost.'

'Oh, Dad!' Joan didn't know whether to laugh or cry with exasperation. 'Well, you'd better take Kevin. He's falling asleep.' Kevin was still sitting on Mackey's lap, but he had his thumb in his mouth, and his eyes kept closing and opening as he battled tiredness. Mr O'Brien took him back to the house.

'We'll keep the sandwiches for later,' Joan decided. 'They might be all we're going to get.'

'But what about our dinners?' Muggins asked.

'What about them?' said Mackey shortly. 'Haven't you just been fed? My ma's sausage rolls were really filling — and we drank gallons of lemonade.'

Muggins was silent for a moment. Then he said, in a small voice, 'I'm dying to go to the loo.'

Mackey snorted. 'Go in the woods, then!'

'That's disgusting!' Joan objected. 'We're meant to be saving the woods, not polluting it.'

'I want to go as well,' Jonathan said sheepishly.

Suddenly, everyone wanted to go.

'If we leave here,' Felicity warned, 'the men will come back and we'll have lost.'

'So what do we do, then?' Jonathan asked.

'I can't hold on any longer,' Muggins wailed.

'Oh, go on, Muggins!' Felicity ordered. 'Go to your house, but be quick. We can only go one by one, and everybody else is waiting.'

Muggins shot off up the lane at great speed.

The gang had barely finished their loo-shuttle when the workmen returned.

'Still here?' the foreman growled.

'What does it look like?' Mackey said cheekily.

The foreman tried a smile. 'Now listen, kids ... what's the point of staying out here all night, in the dark and the cold, when you could be tucked up in your beds? It won't make a difference anyway. That wall will be built whether you like it or not. You might as well give up now. You've made your protest, and we'll pass it on to the Council.'

A voice piped up from behind the foreman. 'You needn't bother. The papers will do that.'

The gang stared in surprise. It was Harold!

The foreman swung around.

Harold was standing in the lane. He looked small and vulnerable.

'And who are you?' the foreman bawled.

'I'm their press agent,' Harold said calmly, staring out the foreman through his gold-rimmed glasses.

'Are you mad?'

Harold raised an eyebrow. 'No, I'm not. But a lot of people will be when they read our story in the papers.'

'I don't believe this!' The foreman was losing his

cool again. He turned to the gang, spread out along the trench. 'What you kids need is a right good thrashing.'

Mackey stood up, fists raised, and danced on the pile of earth. 'Come on, then!' he yelled. 'Thrash me if you dare. Thrash me! What are you waiting for? Come on!'

The workmen started to titter.

The foreman's face darkened. 'I'll put an end to this once and for all,' he muttered. Angrily he strode over to Joan's back gate and went up the garden path.

The gang didn't need to see what was happening, for very soon they could hear. The whole district could hear. Mr O'Brien and the foreman were having a shouting match. The gang couldn't make out the exact sentences, but the word 'police' figured loud and clear on at least two occasions. Mrs McCarthy and Mrs Kelly came out into the garden to see what all the fuss was about, and they joined in the argument over the hedge.

Finally the foreman stomped back out into the lane and headed for the woods, beckoning to his men. 'Right. We'll let the police deal with this one.' He aimed a parting shot at the gang as he went. 'I hope they throw you in jail. See how you like that!'

Then they were gone.

The gang breathed a sigh of relief. It had been terrifying to have to sit there while the foreman raged at them, when all they'd wanted to do was run.

'Well!' said Harold. 'Isn't he a right temper-box?'

'Thanks, Harold,' Felicity said. 'You were really great.'

'Yeah,' Mackey agreed grudgingly.

'Did you mean what you said about being our press agent?' Jonathan asked.

'If you want.'

'What could you do?'

'I could get a reporter here from the *Village News*, and a photographer.'

'That comes out tomorrow,' Orla said. 'It's too late.'

'No it's not. It doesn't hit the shops until afternoon. There's still time to get in a last-minute story.'

'And how can you do that?' Joan demanded. 'They're not going to listen to you.'

'Yes they will,' Harold replied smugly. 'The editor is a friend of my father's. He's always at our house.'

The gang gaped. Harold never ceased to surprise them.

Mackey was excited. 'Hey, that's deadly! You'd better get moving, then.'

Harold looked at them calmly. 'We haven't discussed payment yet.'

'Payment! You want money?' Jonathan exploded.

'Greedy little creep!' Mackey snorted.

'But we haven't got any money,' Muggins wailed.

Harold was unperturbed. 'I don't want money.'

'What do you want, then?' Orla asked testily. She was sucking her broken fingernails, which had begun to throb.

Harold turned to Mackey. 'Where's that place you hid in, last year, when the police were looking for you?'

'The Tunnel! He wants the Tunnel!' Joan squealed in outrage.

'I don't want it. I just want to know where it is.'

'Same thing,' Jonathan said.

'No it's not.'

'Yes it is.'

'Forget it!' Mackey snapped.

'Right, so.' Harold turned and went off up the lane.

'Don't let him go!' Felicity pleaded.

'We don't even want to use the Tunnel any more,' Joan said. 'It's squashy.'

'We used it on Monday.'

'You said yourself it wasn't the same since your mum and the police were there.'

'Harold! Harold!' Felicity screamed. Harold turned

the corner and was gone. 'Don't let him go! We need him! Harold!'

'*Harold*!' Orla, Joan, and Muggins added their voices to Felicity's.

'How does he always get his own way?' Jonathan muttered under his breath.

Mackey was sulking.

Harold appeared in the lane again.

'You win,' Felicity called. 'We'll show you the Tunnel.'

Harold sauntered back to stand in front of them again.

'That's not quite all,' he said.

'What else?' Felicity asked.

'I want Mackey to teach me and Billy and Mark how to do parachute rolls.'

'Why should I teach those brats anything?' Mackey scowled. 'They haven't even come to support our protest.'

'Maybe Harold didn't tell them,' Felicity cut in.

'I did. Billy's in trouble with his mother and she won't let him come up here, and Mark won't come without Billy.'

Mackey was still scowling.

'Any of us can teach you parachute rolls, Harold,' Felicity said.

'I want Mackey. He's the expert.'

'Oh, go on, Mackey!' urged Joan.

'It won't kill you to do it,' Orla said.

'Harold's right, you know,' Felicity put in. 'At least he has the sense to go for the best.'

Mackey eyed Harold. 'A reporter and a photographer ... and we make tomorrow's paper?'

'Yes.'

'OK, then. It's a deal.'

Harold smiled. 'I'll be off, so. Got a lot to do.' He sauntered back down the lane and disappeared around the corner.

The gang slumped back in sheer exhaustion.

'I don't know who's worse — the foreman or Harold,' Jonathan said.

'Harold's worse!' Mackey replied with certainty. 'You never know what he's got in that scheming little mind of his.'

'It's good that he's bringing the photographer, all the same,' Muggins said. 'It'll be a great photo.'

'Photos!' Felicity sat up, tiredness forgotten. 'We need our placards, the ones we made for the march.'

'They're in our shed. I'll get them,' Muggins offered.

'Oh no you won't!' Mackey glared. 'If we start leaving here for whatever we want, it's not a proper sit-in.'

'I'll ask Carly to get them,' Orla suggested. She started to call, 'Carly! Carly!'

At first there was no answer; then Carly's face appeared over the top of the gate.

'What?' she said.

'Carly, pet, you know the placards we made saying "Save Conker Woods"?'

'Yes.'

'They're in the shed. Will you get them and bring them out here to us, please?'

'I can't.'

'Why not?'

'I'm not allowed out of the garden.'

Orla rolled her eyes to heaven. 'I give you permission, Carly. It's all right.'

'You're not Mammy, and Mammy says I can't.' With that, Carly got down off the gate and was gone.

'Carly! *Carly!*' Orla roared, but Carly didn't come back.

'That maddening child!' Orla said in exasperation.

Felicity was laughing. 'She had you there, Orla!'

'I'll get them myself.' Orla got up from the trench, turning to Mackey as she did so. 'And don't you argue. We need those placards.'

Mackey said nothing.

Orla was back in a couple of minutes with the placards. She handed one to each of the gang.

'This'll be brilliant for the photo,' Jonathan enthused.

It did indeed look brilliant — the raw pile of earth, the backdrop of trees, and the six of them with their placards held high: 'Save Conker Woods', 'County Council Keep Out!', 'Save Conker Woods'.

Mackey grinned. 'Just wait till everyone sees us in the paper tomorrow!'

☆   ☆   ☆

The photographer came at a quarter to five. She quickly took six or seven shots from different angles, wrote down the gang's names, then departed.

'Is that all?' Mackey shouted after her, outraged.

'Reporter'll be along soon,' the photographer shouted back.

They waited.

It was half past five before the reporter showed up, but he was all business. Using a tape recorder, and making the odd note in a jotter, he got the story out of them. They all had their say. Felicity, in particular, was concerned that he should understand about the Red Belly and how important it was to them.

'It's always been there for us,' she told him. 'Even when I was very small, I always wanted to climb it.'

'You took long enough about that, Sis!' grinned Jonathan.

'Well, I did it, though, didn't I?' said Felicity defensively.

'Don't mind him,' Orla advised her.

'Go on,' the reporter said.

Felicity tried to explain. 'It's our gang headquarters, but it's much, much more. It's our second home. It's where we can go to be by ourselves, where adults can't follow us. Up there, the only rules are ours. We keep things in the Crow's Nest, secret things .... And up high it's really dangerous, but we know how to deal with that. We've learnt. It's like being on top of the world — everything else is at our feet: the sea, the city, the airport, all the houses ....'

'The church spire isn't at our feet,' objected Muggins.

'Well, you know what I mean,' Felicity said. 'Oh, it's coming out all wrong!'

The reporter grinned. 'Don't worry. I get the drift.'

'The Red Belly is the most important thing in the whole woods,' Felicity persisted. 'We want to keep it for the children of Conker Road — the children coming after us — so that they can enjoy it like we do.'

'You're going to let them all up there with you?'

Felicity was taken aback. 'Well, not now. They're too small. In a few years ... when they're bigger.'

'And you won't want it yourselves then?'

'Yes, we will! We'll always want the Red Belly!'

'It'll get a bit crowded up there, so.'

Felicity struggled to answer, but the reporter grinned again. 'Sorry. Just teasing!' He switched off his tape recorder and slapped the jotter shut. 'I think I've got enough now.'

'Will it definitely be in the paper tomorrow?' Jonathan asked.

The reporter nodded. 'Good luck with your sit-in tonight,' he said. 'Wouldn't fancy it myself. Looks like rain, too.' With a wave, he departed down the lane and was gone.

Felicity was upset. 'I couldn't explain properly,' she fretted. 'All that bit about the Red Belly .... I tried to tell him, but it came out sounding stupid!'

'No it didn't,' Joan said loyally.

'It did!' Felicity couldn't be consoled. 'It's really difficult to explain about things you feel deep inside, isn't it?'

'Yeah,' said Mackey softly. 'Yeah, it is.'

'Food!' screeched Muggins, pointing. 'Food!'

Mrs Duggan was coming up the lane, carrying a big roasting-tin. Behind her, Mrs Kelly carried a pile of plates. Carly trotted in front, holding a fistful of forks.

'Dinner,' she announced proudly. 'It's shepherd's pie.'

'Thanks, Carly! Did you cook it all by yourself?' Joan teased.

The little girl was more than able for her. 'I helped,' she said.

The shepherd's pie was dished out, and the gang suddenly found they were ravenous.

'The photographer from the *Village News* was here, Mum,' Jonathan announced, 'and a reporter. We're going to be in the paper tomorrow.'

Mrs Kelly was astonished. 'How did you manage that?'

'Harold arranged it.'

'Mum, you won't forget to take our sleeping-bags out of the attic, will you?' Orla asked.

Mrs Duggan frowned. 'So you're going ahead with it, then?'

'Of course we are!' Muggins said. 'We can't give up now.'

'My ma hasn't been out for ages,' Mackey complained. 'Will you tell her to get my sleeping-bag too?'

'And tell my dad,' Joan added.

Mrs Duggan looked at Mrs Kelly, who sighed. 'I suppose we'd better get them organised.'

Felicity thought of something else. 'And, Mum, can we have the storm lantern we used for our sleep-out last year — the one Dad keeps in the attic?'

'I don't know what your father is going to say about all of this,' Mrs Kelly said.

'You can talk to him.'

'I suppose so.' Mrs Kelly nodded, resigned.

The gang finished their shepherd's pie, licking the plates clean. Mrs Duggan gave them bottles of lemonade, mugs, and an apple each. Then the two women went off with Carly, leaving the gang alone again.

They were in high spirits after the food.

'I think this day is going to last forever,' Felicity said. 'It seems ages ago that we were in old Fitzy's garden.'

'That's because so much has happened since,' Orla said. She was munching away on an apple. Her broken fingernails looked very odd, but she hadn't complained about them once.

'It'll be great sleeping out again,' Jonathan said happily.

'There won't be any more ghosts, will there?' Muggins looked apprehensive.

'Who knows!' said Mackey carelessly. 'Who knows what creatures might come crawling out of the dark of night?'

'Stop!' wailed Muggins. 'Stop!'

'Don't tease him, Mackey,' Orla scolded. 'You know what he's like.'

Mackey grinned. It was going to be a brilliant night.

It was a thoroughly miserable night.

It started well enough. It was light until almost ten o'clock. The gang ate their cheese sandwiches, then found that they were being plied with more food, and drinks, and more food again, by a succession of parents — who tried at the same time to persuade them to come home. The gang resisted all their entreaties. Joan's mum was particularly upset. She seemed to think the whole thing was Joan's dad's fault for encouraging them.

'He didn't, Mum, honest!' Joan insisted. 'He just backed us up when the council men came. He was great!'

As darkness fell, their sleeping-bags and anoraks were finally brought out. It had got quite cool, so the gang were glad of the extra clothing. Mr Kelly had remembered the storm lantern and it cast a bright circle of light in the laneway. The gang were snug and warm, and their spirits were high as they prepared to face whatever the night would bring — to face it by themselves.

But Mackey's mum had other ideas.

She staggered down the garden path, carrying an armchair, which she deposited in the middle of the lane. A couple of folded blankets were on the chair seat. The gang stared, uncomprehending, until Mackey screeched, 'What d'ya think you're doing, Ma?'

'I'm going to keep an eye on you all,' Mrs McCarthy said firmly, starting to unfold the blankets.

'You can't stay here all night, Ma. You just can't!'

'Oh yes I can. I'm not leaving you on your own —

107

that foreman might come back and start bothering you.'

'He won't — not at this hour of night.'

Mrs McCarthy raised her eyebrows. 'So why won't you all come home to sleep?'

''Cause we're having a sit-in ... and you're trying to spoil it all. It's *our* sit-in. We want to do it on our own. We don't *need* to be minded.'

Mrs McCarthy sat down and wrapped the blankets around her knees.

Desperate remedies were called for, and Mackey's tone changed to pleading. '*Please*, Ma!' It wasn't easy to get his mother to change her mind at the best of times.

Felicity decided to come to Mackey's aid. 'It's not that we don't want you, Mrs McCarthy. It's really nice of you to offer to sit up with us. But we started the protest, and we've got to see it through by ourselves. We're all old enough to be responsible about things.'

Mrs McCarthy raised her eyebrows, amused.

Orla quickly added her voice to the argument. 'Couldn't you stay in the house, Mrs McCarthy, and if there's a problem we'll come and fetch you? There's no need for you to sit out here in the dark and cold just because we have to.'

'Yes,' agreed Jonathan. 'That doesn't make sense.'

'And we want to be on our own,' Muggins said.

Mrs McCarthy was frowning. 'Well, I don't know .... I promised the others that I'd keep an eye on you.'

'You can do that from the house, Mrs McCarthy,' Joan said. 'I'm sure my dad will be watching too.'

'And mine,' Jonathan said.

Mrs McCarthy considered this for a moment, un-decided, then said, 'You promise to call at the first sign of trouble?'

'Yeah, Ma, of course!' Mackey agreed with relief.

'We'll be all right, Mrs McCarthy,' Orla reassured her. 'Really we will.'

Mrs McCarthy was still worried. 'The back door will be open. If you need anything at all, just come on in. I'll be in the dining-room. I'm not going to bed.'

Mackey beamed. They'd won! 'Thanks, Ma.'

Mrs McCarthy picked up the armchair. 'If you're quite sure you'll be OK ....'

'We will!' the gang chorused.

'Have a good night, then.' Mrs McCarthy headed off up the garden path with her chair. After a minute or so they heard the back door being shut.

'Phew! That was a close one!' Mackey exploded. 'I thought she'd refuse to go — she can be fierce stubborn.'

'She nearly spoilt everything,' Jonathan said. 'Imagine having her here minding us like babies!'

They settled down for the long night ahead.

It was strange sitting in the lane by lamplight, but they were veterans of such things since their sleep-out under the Red Belly.

'Nobody's to mention ghosts,' said Joan firmly.

Mackey stretched his mouth into a fierce grin. 'It's coming to take you away, ha-ha!' he croaked.

'Shut up, Mackey. Shut *up*!' Joan put her hands over her ears.

'Give over, Mackey! We've had enough of ghosts,' Jonathan said. 'We don't want to spoil our sit-in.'

'OK, OK!' Mackey put up his hands in surrender.

They sat and talked, the dark woods looming overhead, the lamplight on their faces, and for a while it was fun — until tiredness hit them. One by one they kept toppling over, as they dozed off sitting up.

Finally Joan said, 'We should go to sleep in shifts, like they do on a ship. Three of us could keep watch for an hour while the other three sleep. Then we'd wake the others and go to sleep ourselves. We'll never last the night as it is. Remember the haunted gate-lodge? We couldn't even keep awake there.'

They had a problem, and they knew it. They decided to adopt Joan's suggestion. After some argument, Felicity, Muggins and Mackey lay down to sleep while Joan, Jonathan and Orla kept watch. At one o'clock they changed shifts.

At half past one it started to rain.

At first it didn't matter, as the trees overhanging the lane kept them dry. But after a while the rain started to seep through, in large drops that fell faster and faster, until they were all thoroughly awake and getting quite uncomfortable.

At two o'clock Mrs McCarthy rushed out with a load of black plastic refuse sacks. She briskly dispensed them in twos to the gang, with orders to pull one over each of their sleeping-bags. They discovered she'd torn a large hole in each of the other sacks, so that when they pulled them on over their heads, down over their anoraks, they could look out through the holes — completely protected from the weather.

Mrs McCarthy fussed around for ages, complaining that they should have come in to wake her at the first sign of rain. Mackey began to think that they'd never get rid of her. However, having checked that they were now protected from the elements, she reluctantly went back into her house again.

'Bloody nuisance!' Mackey grumbled.

'She's not a nuisance,' Orla said. 'She's really nice to be thinking about us at all. I'm glad she brought the plastic sacks — we'd have been soaked through by morning.'

'I suppose so,' Mackey admitted, somewhat ungraciously. Privately he wished that it was someone else's ma who was fussing.

They tried to go back to their shift arrangements for sleep, but found that they kept waking up, as the rain was getting heavier and heavier and drumming on the

plastic bags. Also, the plastic made them sweat after a while, and they got sticky and uncomfortable. By half past three they were thoroughly miserable, and no one was asleep.

The storm lantern cast a watery light as the rain and the darkness pressed in all around them. The placards lay in a sodden mass — nobody had thought to put them in a plastic bag too. The loose soil in the trench had become saturated, and it gradually turned to mud which subsided beneath the gang, so that each of them now sat in a little hollow which collected rain.

The mud got over everything. It covered the plastic sacks. It caked their hands. It stuck to their faces, when they tried to lie on their sides to protect themselves from the rain. It half-blinded them when they rubbed their eyes with tiredness. It clung to Joan's hair in lumps where she had swatted at something crawling along her forehead.

'I didn't think it was going to be like this,' she complained. 'I didn't think it would be this bad.'

'Well, I can't help it if it rains,' Mackey said reasonably.

'I'm tired of sitting up,' Muggins whinged, 'but there's nowhere left to lie down any more. It's all gooey!'

'Mud, mud, glorious mud!' sang Orla, giggling hysterically. 'Just look! We're sinking by the hour. We'll be buried up to our necks by morning.'

'We could move over onto the lane,' suggested Jonathan. 'At least we'd be out of the mud.'

'We'd be out of the shelter of the trees then,' Felicity pointed out. 'It's absolutely bucketing rain — I know we're wet, but the trees are still keeping the worst of it off.'

'No they're not,' Jonathan scoffed. 'It's like sitting underneath a sieve!'

'We're staying right here,' Mackey declared firmly. 'This trench is what we're defending. Either we do it right or we don't do it at all. Anybody who can't take the discomfort, just go home to bed!'

There was a short silence, but no one took Mackey up on the offer.

'It's nearly four o'clock,' Felicity said. 'What time is dawn?'

The notion of dawn cheered them up a bit.

'I think it's five o'clock,' said Mackey, 'or even before five .... It's not far away, anyhow.'

'Maybe your mum will bring us some breakfast then,' Muggins said hopefully.

Dawn ... breakfast .... Things could only get better.

'It's not a proper sit-in if you don't have hardship, anyway,' Mackey declared. 'You're meant to suffer for a cause if you really believe in it.'

'We're doing that, all right,' sighed Orla.

'We should be proud of ourselves, then,' said Mackey.

By ten past four, the rain had eased off to a thin drizzle. By the time a dismal dawn crept in, it had stopped completely.

The gang sat and listened as the birds grew restless in the grey half-light. They were restless themselves, and bone-weary; they were too tired even to sleep. The plastic bags encasing them were firmly stuck in the mud — but at least they still kept the sleeping-bags dry.

'How about three cheers for us?' Felicity suggested wearily. 'At least we've made it through the night.'

'Shh! What's that?' Mackey interrupted.

They listened.

The low throbbing sound of an engine in the distance came slowly closer ... and closer ....

'It's in the lane,' Mackey hissed.

Fully alert, they watched and waited.

The JCB swung around the corner and stopped, its lights trained on the filled-in trench. Behind the JCB came the foreman, on foot. When he saw the gang he paused for a moment, startled to find them still sitting there. But, recovering his composure quickly, he signalled to the JCB driver.

The driver put down the JCB's supports and pulled on some levers. The digging scoop went into action, biting deeply into the soil of the trench.

Mackey went into action too.

He was out of his sleeping-bag in a flash. Racing down the side of the trench, he threw himself on top of the earth that the JCB was about to lift. The next instant, he was several feet in the air as the scoop rose again.

Then it stopped. Some of the muddy, heaped-up soil went sliding to the ground. Mackey clung to the teeth of the scoop, trying to stop himself from sliding off too.

The JCB driver was agitated. He opened the door of the cab to consult with the foreman; but before he could speak, Felicity, horrified at what was happening, had gone into action too.

She attacked the foreman with her fists, beating fiercely against his big chest and screaming, 'Put Mackey down! Put him *down*!'

Orla raced over to stop Felicity, frantic in case the foreman hurt her. Mackey, meanwhile, was screeching encouragement from his precarious position up on the scoop. 'Thump him, Felicity! Thump him!'

Orla reached Felicity and managed to pull her away. Then, steaming with anger, she turned on the foreman. 'What are you doing?' she shouted. 'I can't *believe* the Council gave you permission to carry on like this.'

The foreman's face told her clearly that she had hit a weak spot. 'They don't know, do they?' Orla went on incredulously. 'The Council don't even know that you're here!'

The JCB driver still had the cab door open. He looked alarmed at Orla's words.

'Hey, John!' he called to the foreman. 'You said they knew. You said this was all official.'

The foreman, furious, didn't answer.

The driver slammed the cab door. Working at his levers, he lowered Mackey and the pile of muddy earth, ever so gently, back onto the trench. Carefully he slid the scoop out from beneath them and swung it into the air. Then he was reversing angrily back up the lane towards Conker Road.

The foreman glared at the gang for a moment, speechless with rage, then turned and followed the JCB.

'Up the Red Belly!' screamed Mackey, sticking a jubilant fist into the air. 'Up the Red Belly!'

The rest of the gang were out of their sleeping-bags now, and they danced around the lane, hugging and laughing and crying, hardly able to believe that they'd won the battle.

'What's going on?' Mrs McCarthy stood by her gate, staring at them in sleepy alarm.

'We won, Ma! We won!' Mackey crowed.

'Was that an engine I heard?' his mother demanded. 'Was somebody here?'

'The foreman came ... with the JCB ... and they tried to dig us out ....' Muggins was almost hysterical as he tried to tell the tale. 'They dug Mackey into the air ... and Felicity attacked the foreman and Orla frightened them off .... And now they're gone for good. We won! We won!'

Mrs McCarthy was upset, and angry. 'You promised you'd come for me if there was trouble, Ignatius. You promised!'

'There wasn't time, Ma,' Mackey insisted.

'There really wasn't, Mrs McCarthy,' Felicity backed him up. 'It all happened so quickly.'

'I'd never have left you alone if I thought something like this would happen. You'd no business trying to face it on your own. You might have been hurt.'

'It's all right, Mrs McCarthy,' Orla soothed her. 'We

told you we were responsible enough to cope, and we did.'

Mrs McCarthy, exasperated, surveyed the mess in the lane — the wet, the mud, the dismal dripping trees, the disintegrating placards, the sleeping-bags sucked down into the muck of the trench, the incredibly filthy gang. Then she looked at the bright, jubilant faces before her, and she sighed. 'Well, it's done now, I suppose. You'll be coming in for breakfast, so?'

'No, we won't, Ma!' Mackey protested. 'And you're not to start all that again. We've won a battle, not the war. Our sit-in is still on.' With that, he climbed back into his sleeping-bag.

'You're wet and dirty, Ignatius!' Mrs McCarthy scolded. 'At least come home and change.'

Mackey shook his head. 'It's only mud. I'm not really wet, and the sleeping-bags are still dry.' He stared at the rest of the gang. Taking the hint, they got into their sleeping-bags too, muddy shoes and all.

Mrs McCarthy shook her head as if she had given up. She turned and went back into the house.

'She could at least have offered us breakfast,' Muggins groaned. 'I'm starving.'

They were all starving, and, now that they'd been out of their sleeping-bags, they were cold as well. It was spitting slightly, threatening to rain again. A light wind had blown up, rustling the leaves of the trees above them and sending showers of water down in huge droplets.

They were just starting to feel sorry for themselves when Mackey's mum returned with six mugs of steaming tea.

'Get that inside you, now,' she said. 'Pancakes following in a few minutes.'

'Hey, thanks, Mrs McCarthy,' Jonathan said. 'You're deadly.'

Mrs McCarthy laughed.

'Yeah — thanks, Ma!' Mackey was relieved that she hadn't just gone off and left them.

Ten minutes later, they were sitting there with plates of big, thick pancakes in front of them. Mrs McCarthy had made each pancake the full size of her big frying-pan, dribbled golden syrup over it, then rolled it up so that it could be eaten in the hands.

'Yummy-yummy!' Muggins sighed blissfully.

'These are gorgeous, Mackey,' said Joan, in between mouthfuls.

'I'm nice and warm again,' Jonathan declared.

'So am I,' Orla said, well contented.

'I'm stuffed!' Felicity, halfway through her last pancake, suddenly found herself full.

They were all stuffed. The empty plates and mugs were passed along and left in a neat pile beside the trench.

'My mum should be up by now,' Joan remarked. 'I hope she comes to see me before she goes to work.'

'Mine too,' said Jonathan, 'and my dad.'

'My mum'll have been up for ages by now,' Orla said. 'The little ones always have her awake at dawn. I'm surprised she hasn't been out here already.'

'You'd think they'd be worried enough to come and check on us.' Joan sounded disgruntled.

'We didn't *want* them to check on us,' Mackey pointed out.

'I know .... But you'd think they would all the same. Anything could have happened to us.'

'Bet my ma phoned the others,' Mackey reckoned.

And so she had, as it turned out. Joan's mum came to see them for a few minutes before she hurried off to work. Jonathan and Felicity's parents came too, and Orla and Muggins's dad.

Finally they were all gone, and the gang were left on their own again.

'Now for Day Two of our sit-in,' Mackey announced.

'It won't be Day Two until lunch-time,' Joan reminded him.

Jonathan groaned. 'Oh, no! It's not even twenty-four hours yet .... It feels like a week!'

The gang were silent. What if the sit-in *did* last that long? They'd just gone through a horribly uncomfortable night, sitting out in the pouring rain, tired, muddy, and harassed by council workers. Would they be able for a whole week of that? Or even more than a week?

It was a daunting thought.

At nine o'clock it started to rain again. No glimmer of sun had shown its face to warm up the day, so the gang stayed in their sleeping-bags. Besides, it was the only way to keep dry. They quickly pulled the plastic sacks over their heads again and stared out at the rain through the holes cut in the front.

They were seriously tired.

The euphoria of the battle they'd won at dawn had kept them going for hours, but now they realised how little sleep they'd had — and just sitting here on the trench was intensely boring. So when Mr O'Brien stood at the back door and started calling, 'Joanie ... oh, Joanie!', Joan was only too glad of the excuse to disappear home for a while.

'I have to go,' she argued. 'Kevin needs me. Anyway, I'm dying to go to the loo.'

Mackey wouldn't let anyone else move until Joan came back, which wasn't for ages.

'You took your time,' he growled at her.

Joan shrugged and looked with distaste at her muddy sleeping-bag before reluctantly climbing back in.

Muggins wanted to go to the loo now, and, having declared that he couldn't hold on another second, was allowed to sprint off home. He was away for half an hour. Mackey was threatening to go and fetch him back when he finally appeared.

One by one, the rest of them paid their visits of necessity, and found it was painfully hard to return to the muck of the laneway. But return they did.

Mackey was furious. 'My ma's gone back to bed!' he complained.

'Well, she *was* up most of the night,' Orla said.

'So were we! Now who's going to bring us tea and stuff?'

'Ungrateful wretch!' Orla said. 'Your mum's fed us already today.'

'Some things are more important than eating — that's what you said yesterday,' Joan reminded him.

'Yesterday was yesterday,' growled Mackey. 'I can change my mind, can't I?'

Things got a bit better when Mrs Duggan appeared with tea and sandwiches. The little ones trailed after her, well wrapped up in raincoats and wellies. At least eating and drinking gave the gang something to do, and banished the tiredness for a while — though the sandwiches quickly got soaked with the rain.

By twelve o'clock, Muggins and Joan were fast asleep, and the rest of them were finding it increasingly hard to keep awake. The rain came down in a steady stream and the trench was running with mud. They were hot, sticky, tired and miserable.

Mackey's mum brought them out big bowls of spaghetti bolognese at one o'clock.

'Let Columbus out for a while, will you, Ma?' Mackey pleaded. 'I miss him.'

'I'll do no such thing,' Mrs McCarthy said. 'I wouldn't put a dog out in this weather. As a matter of fact ....' She was going to say something else, but instead she pulled her raincoat around her and hurried off back to the house again.

The gang discovered they were too tired even to eat. Muggins buried his food in the mud and went back to sleep. Joan refused to wake up at all. Felicity found herself dozing as she tried to eat, waking with a start to find her nose buried in her spaghetti. Mackey picked at the food without enthusiasm. Jonathan and Orla desperately tried to keep awake by having a daft competition to see who could find the longest piece of spaghetti.

By two o'clock, exhaustion had them all toppling over at regular intervals. Mackey said angrily, 'Just look at us! One day — *one* day — and we can't take it. Wake up, everyone! Wake up, Muggins! Wake up, Joan!' He leaned over and pulled at Joan's plastic bag.

She groaned sleepily, then woke up in alarm. 'What's wrong? What's wrong?' She sat up and looked around, rubbing her eyes.

Jonathan shook Muggins. 'Wake up, Muggins. Come on, wake up!' Muggins attempted to open his eyes.

'Fine sentries you pair would make in an army!' Mackey said scathingly.

'Sentries shouldn't have to be on duty for twenty-four hours,' Joan replied crossly.

'We should sing or something,' Felicity suggested. 'It would keep us awake.'

'Hey, that's a great idea,' Mackey agreed. 'What'll we sing?'

'Something to inspire us.'

They thought hard, but they couldn't think of a suitable song until Muggins, still half asleep, offered, 'What about "Rudolph the Red-Nosed Reindeer"?'

'Don't be stupid, Muggins!' Orla said, exasperated. 'That's a Christmas song.'

But Mackey was laughing hysterically, like it was the funniest thing he'd ever heard. When he'd recovered a bit, he gasped, 'No, it's perfect — just perfect ... very inspirational! Good old Muggins! Come on, everybody, let's sing!'

He launched into the first verse. 'Rudolph the red-nosed reindeer had a very shiny nose ....'

The rest of them joined in with gusto, and Conker Lane resounded with their voices.

They finished the song, and Mackey shouted, 'Again!'

They sang it a second time, even louder, then a third time. They were enjoying themselves, and they didn't feel tired any more. As the rain poured down relentlessly, forming lakes around them, they shouted and yelled and sang — 'Rudolph with your nose so bright, won't you guide my sleigh tonight?'

By the time they'd been through the song a dozen times, they were in a high good humour and ready to face anything.

'Hey! Action stations!' Mackey warned suddenly. 'There's a posse coming.'

'Oh-oh ... I don't like the look of this,' Orla said.

A forest of umbrellas was moving up Mackey's garden path and out into the lane. Mrs McCarthy was in the lead. Behind her was Mrs Duggan, with all the children. Carly and Conor had their own umbrellas. Mrs Duggan was carrying Aisling in her arms, while holding a big golf umbrella; Shane was clinging to her legs. Joan's dad had Kevin in tow. Even more ominous, both Mr and Mrs Kelly were there too.

'What's Dad doing home at this hour of the day?' Jonathan whispered to Felicity. 'It's only three o'clock.'

'And Mum's been home for ages,' Felicity whispered back. 'Why didn't she come and see us before now?'

The group came to a halt in front of the gang. It was obvious that nobody wanted to be the first to speak. Finally, Mrs McCarthy appointed herself their spokesperson.

'I'm glad you're all in such good form,' she said, 'for we've got bad news.'

'What kind of bad news?' Mackey asked in alarm.

Mrs McCarthy waved an envelope in the air. 'Know what this is?'

The gang stared at the envelope, wondering what

was coming. Mackey said testily, 'Yeah, we've all got X-ray vision.'

'It's an injunction,' Mrs McCarthy went on, ignoring Mackey's sarcasm. 'The County Council went to court this morning, and this is a court order, from a judge, ordering you to stop interfering with the building of this wall.'

'Good,' Mackey retorted. 'At least somebody's taking notice.'

'No, it's not good,' Mrs McCarthy told him firmly. 'It's over! You can't disobey a court order.'

'Just watch me!' Mackey declared with relish.

'Why did they just make a court order against Mackey?' Muggins demanded indignantly.

'They didn't,' Mrs Duggan broke in. 'I have one too. We all got them.'

Mr Kelly shook his envelope at Felicity and Jonathan. 'This is serious stuff, make no mistake about it. I left work as soon as I heard. You'll have to stop your protest or we'll have the police here by tea-time.'

'We don't care about court orders,' Jonathan said hotly.

'Let them put us in jail!' Mackey shouted. 'I'm willing to go to jail.'

'So am I,' yelled Muggins.

'Well, *I'm* not,' Mrs McCarthy said sharply. 'You just don't get the picture, do you? *You* won't go to jail — *we* will. The court orders are against us, as your parents.'

'Well, I'm not giving up,' Mackey said flatly.

'Nor me,' said Felicity, outraged.

'You can't make us give up now,' said Joan. 'We won't give up!'

'Now, Joanie, be reasonable,' Mr O'Brien pleaded.

'The *Village News* is out today,' Felicity suddenly remembered. 'It'll support us.'

Mackey's mum sighed. 'Look, kids, you've made

your point. I'm sorry it's turned out like this. We'll give you time to talk it through, but you don't really have a choice. You'll have to come in.'

The gang were silent, angry.

Mr Kelly was whispering to Mrs McCarthy. She nodded, then eyed the other parents, and one by one they moved off home, without any more attempts to persuade the gang. The Duggan children headed for their back gate, stamping gleefully through the puddles in the laneway.

Mr Kelly was back in a few minutes with a copy of the *Village News*. 'I got it on the way home from work,' he explained.

He handed Jonathan a huge umbrella. 'You'll need this to hold over the paper, or it'll be soaked before you can read it.'

'Thanks, Dad!' Felicity took the paper, excited, and stared at the front page. There was no mention of them there.

'You're in it all right,' Mr Kelly said. He seemed about to add something else, but thought better of it. He turned to go. 'Don't be too long about coming in, will you?' He went off down the lane.

'Are they all deaf or something?' Mackey demanded. 'We told them we weren't moving!'

'Let's see the paper.' Orla scrambled out of her sleeping-bag and crouched behind Felicity. Joan and Muggins did the same. They peered over Felicity's shoulder as Jonathan held the brolly over the lot of them.

'We're not even on the front page!' Mackey complained. 'You'd think we'd be important enough for the front.'

Felicity was turning the pages. 'Not on page 2, either,' she said.

Page 3 was all advertisements. Page 4 ... page 5 ....

'Here we are,' she said, disappointed.

They stared at the page. Their photograph was down at the bottom, and there was a small write-up, to one side, headed 'Conker Woods Sit-In'.

'Our placards look great,' Mackey said.

'That's about all,' said Felicity grimly. 'You can hardly even make out our faces — it's not a very good photo.'

'Read what it says,' Orla urged her. 'I can't see it properly from here.'

Felicity read:

The children of Conker Road held a sit-in yesterday in Conker Lane. They are protesting over a wall being built by the County Council which will restrict access to Conker Woods. Their spokesperson, Ms Felicity Kelly, said, 'We've always played in Conker Woods. The Council can't take it away from us now.'

'Hey!' Mackey said. 'You're not the spokesperson — I am. I organised all this.'

'I didn't ask them to say that,' said Felicity crossly.

'Go on!' urged Joan.

Felicity continued to read.

A spokesperson for the County Council said today, 'We're not taking all the woods, only half of it. This will form the grounds of the new Conker Woods Retirement Home. Old people have needs too. The children will still have the other half to play in, and we're leaving full access to this from Conker Lane.'

Felicity stopped.

'Go on!' Orla said.

'That's all.'

'That's *all*?'

Felicity nodded, too angry to speak.

'It can't be,' said Orla. 'Here, give me the paper.' She leaned forward and grabbed it from Felicity. She and Jonathan and Muggins read the article for themselves.

'They're not even on our side!' said Jonathan, outraged. 'They've given the County Council the last word.'

'That reporter was here for ages,' Mackey said indignantly. 'Why did he bother, if he wasn't going to tell our story?'

'He never even mentioned the Red Belly,' Felicity fretted. 'I tried to explain how important it is, but he didn't listen ....'

'Wait till I get Harold!' Mackey growled.

'It's not his fault,' Orla said. 'He kept his end of the bargain. That reporter just didn't report things properly.'

Jonathan grabbed the paper, scrunched it into a ball, and flung it down the lane. 'Stupid paper!' he shouted.

Joan got out of her sleeping-bag and stood up. 'Well, that's it,' she said. 'Nobody cares. But if I stay here, the police will come and take my dad away, and who'll look after Kevin then? Mackey's mum was right. It's all over.'

She pulled her sleeping-bag from the mud with a loud squelch, and started dragging it towards her garden gate.

The rest of the gang sat staring after her.

Nobody spoke for a few minutes. The rain still poured down, hopping off the gravel of the laneway and drumming on the plastic sacks. They were sick of the very sound of it.

Finally Orla said, 'What about *our* little ones? If the police take my mum and dad away to prison, what will happen to them? Maybe they'll be taken to prison too ....'

'The police wouldn't do that,' Jonathan said, sounding unsure.

'They'd be taken into care,' said Mackey, 'to a children's home. Fella in the pub told me about it.'

'You mean an *orphanage*?' exclaimed Orla in alarm. 'But they'd be terrified! Carly won't ever go to sleep without a kiss from my mum — and Conor needs his special teddy ....' She grabbed hold of her sleeping-bag and shook her head at the others. 'Sorry ... I just can't let that happen.' She yanked the bag out of the trench and trailed it down the lane towards home.

Muggins was up in an instant. 'Wait for me!' he called.

Felicity and Mackey and Jonathan watched them go, knowing it was all over.

'We've lost,' said Jonathan mournfully. 'After all that, we've lost.'

'At least we tried.' Felicity, attempting to sound cheerful, failed miserably.

Mackey stared at the rain pelting relentlessly down, at the laneway running with mud from the trench, at the sodden remains of their precious placards, at the sopping muck which threatened to swallow them up; and he hunched his shoulders in defeat.

'Let's go home,' he said.

The next morning, the gang sat up in the cherry tree by Mackey's back gate, watching the council men set to work.

It was a beautiful day. The rain had cleared within hours of the gang abandoning their sit-in.

'Typical!' Mackey snorted. 'Even the weather was against us.' He glared down the lane at the JCB, which was preparing to dig out the trench. The foreman and the grey-haired man stood to one side. 'I bet they're gloating at us.' Mackey's mind was filled with thoughts of revenge.

'They're not even looking this way,' Jonathan pointed out.

'I don't think they've noticed us,' Felicity said.

'They're deliberately ignoring us,' insisted Mackey.

'Oh, what does it matter now, anyway?' Joan said, exasperated.

Mackey scowled. 'It matters.'

The JCB made short work of clearing the trench. Soon the hole was cut again, sharp and deep, and the earth was piled up against the trees at the edge of Conker Woods. The JCB came to a halt by the Duggans' gate, and the driver got down to join the others. The foreman took out a mobile phone.

'Shh!' Mackey hissed. The gang strained to hear what he was saying.

'We're ready to pour concrete. Now look here, we can't wait — those infernal kids are still around .... Right .... Right .... OK, then, if that's the best you can do ....'

The foreman put the mobile away in his pocket and made a face at the waiting men. 'The ready-mix will be here at half past twelve.'

'That's over two hours away!' the grey-haired man protested.

'I know ....' The foreman stood and looked at the trench with a frown on his face.

Mackey was rubbing his hands in glee. He beckoned to the others to move close, so he could whisper to them.

'They'll be going for their tea-break,' he grinned. 'We'll be able to knock the clay in again.'

'We can't,' Joan said firmly. 'They'll put our folks in jail.'

'But they won't know it's us, will they?' Mackey said triumphantly. 'I mean, they won't be able to *prove* anything — not if they don't see us doing it.'

'They'll know anyway,' said Jonathan.

'Yeah, but knowing and proving are two different things. Can you imagine them in court? No, yer honour, we didn't actually *see* the kids filling in the trench ....' Mackey laughed.

'He's right, you know,' Orla chuckled.

The gang perked up. The injunction had been a bitter blow. Maybe they could get their own back — even if it did only delay things for a while.

'I'd give anything to see their faces if they found the trench filled in again,' Felicity declared.

'We won't have time to fill it all in,' Joan objected. 'They'll only be gone for half an hour.'

'We will if they stay away until half past twelve,' Mackey pointed out.

'Let's do it!' Jonathan said. Muggins was nodding enthusiastically too.

Mackey smirked.

They settled down to wait. The men were sitting in the lane, on some building blocks that had been dug up out of the trench. They sat there talking and smoking, their backs turned to the gang.

At half past ten the grey-haired man got up and went off through the woods. The foreman and the JCB driver were still talking.

'I wish they'd hurry up and go,' whispered Mackey impatiently.

But the men showed no signs of moving.

Eventually, the grey-haired man came back, carrying the big black kettle they'd seen at the gate-lodge the week before. The kettle was steaming. He also carried a plastic supermarket bag. He put the kettle down, took three huge mugs out of the bag, and poured dark tea straight from the kettle into the mugs. Then he produced a carton of milk and a large pack of Kimberley biscuits, which he opened and passed around.

The gang felt their mouths watering.

'I'm hungry,' Muggins complained, holding his stomach.

'They're not moving at all,' Joan said in disgust.

'There goes our last chance of getting our own back,' Jonathan sighed.

Mackey glowered.

The workmen still gave no sign of being aware of the gang up the tree.

'Hey, Mackey, look!' Felicity nudged Mackey and pointed.

Up at the other end of the lane, a shadowy figure slunk quietly from the woods. It was Columbus — with a very rotten-looking rat clutched in his jaws. He headed towards Mackey's back gate, then stopped as he spotted the men. He also spotted something else.

Kimberley biscuits! His favourites!

Columbus took off towards the men, wagging his tail. The men never even noticed him until he was on top of them. Columbus dropped his rat and lunged for the biscuits. The rat fell into the foreman's steaming mug of tea.

Screams of rage were followed by gagging sounds. The men had their hands to their noses as the scalding tea intensified the smell of decomposing rat. Columbus scarpered with the entire packet of biscuits, jumping over the trench and the piled-up earth to disappear into the woods with his prize.

The gang dropped quickly out of the tree, fled up Mackey's garden path, and hid in the shed. They listened to the commotion in the laneway.

'We can't stay here!' Joan hissed. 'They'll find us.'

'They don't know which house is mine,' Mackey said.

'Yes they do! They're not stupid!'

'Columbus will come back when he's finished the biscuits,' Muggins moaned. 'They'll follow him in here.'

'Muggins is right,' Felicity agreed. 'We're sitting ducks.'

'Let's get out of here,' Orla said.

'But we can't go back into the lane!' Joan cried.

'We can go through Mackey's house.'

'My ma'll see us!' Mackey squealed.

'Can't be helped.' Orla was all practical now. 'We rush in the back door, up the hall, and out the front door before she can stop us.'

'She'll kill me!' wailed Mackey.

'Well, it's either her or the foreman — take your pick.'

Mackey hopped from one leg to the other in an agony of indecision. A roar from the direction of the lane made up his mind for him. 'OK. Follow me!'

The gang burst out of the shed and in through Mackey's kitchen door. They were up the hall and had the front door open before Mrs McCarthy came running down the stairs.

'Ignatius? Ignatius! What's going on? Come back! Come back!'

Mrs McCarthy stood at the front door and watched in fury as the gang disappeared at top speed down Conker Road.

They ran and ran, until they reached the entrance to the old estate. They went in and up the avenue without stopping. They were puffing and panting, getting seriously short of breath. Muggins had a stitch in his side and lagged behind, wailing, 'Wait, will you. Wait!'

But survival instincts kept them all running until they could find a safe place to hide. They crawled in under one of the tree-tents and collapsed on the ground, hidden from the world outside. No one would find them here.

They struggled to regain their breaths. It was a long time before anybody spoke. Then Felicity gasped, 'I don't care what happens to us ... it was worth it.'

'It won't happen to you, it'll happen to me!' Mackey said.

'Did you see the men's faces?' Jonathan gloated.

'That awful pong! We could even smell it up the tree!' Joan put her hands over her nose, as if the smell was still around.

'Columbus was brilliant!' Muggins declared.

'He was, too,' Felicity giggled. 'How could we ever have thought up a revenge as deadly as that?'

Mackey was smiling now, unable to help himself. 'Yeah,' he said proudly, 'he was good, all right.'

They sat on the branches of the tree-tent and talked for ages — until Jonathan said, 'It's half past twelve. They'll be pouring the concrete.'

The rest of the gang went quiet. It was like having a minute's silence to mark the end of their battle for the woods. They had fought and they had lost. The foundations of the wall were in place. There was nothing more they could do.

None of the gang went near the woods for the next few days. With all the excitement over, the reality of what had happened was beginning to sink in. The concrete strip seared Conker Lane like a living gash.

They couldn't bear to go near the Red Belly — it only reminded them of what they were losing. Mackey went to stay with his dad in the pub for a few days. Orla started her vanishing-up-to-the-village trick again.

On Sunday, Jonathan and Muggins went to see Dara's granny. None of the gang had received a letter from Zambia recently, and they wanted to find out if she had any news. She hadn't, but she was expecting a letter giving details of Dara's return flight any day. Joan stayed at home, looking after Kevin, as he was being troublesome with teething. Felicity took Tiggy and Scut for long walks by herself. She tried to persuade Joan to come with her and bring Columbus, but Joan only screeched, 'You must be joking! *He*'d bring *me* for a walk. I'd spend the whole time digging my heels in. No, thanks!'

On Monday afternoon, Joan and Felicity took Kevin walking on Conker Road, each holding a tiny hand. He couldn't go very far at a time, but they managed to tire him out thoroughly. On Tuesday morning, Joan said he'd slept right through the night for the first time since the previous Friday. So they walked him up and down the road again, hoping to repeat the miracle.

Later, trying to keep as busy as possible, Felicity took Tiggy and Scut for a long trek right to the top of the old estate — a distance of well over a mile. Up until then, Felicity had steadfastly refused even to think about the Red Belly. Now the dammed-up feelings came rushing back, threatening to overwhelm her. A deep ache inside her grew and grew as the coming loss of their beloved tree finally hit home. Tiggy and Scut sensed her distress and hovered anxiously around her.

'It's OK,' Felicity sobbed. 'I'll be all right in a minute.'

She sat down on a grassy bank and hugged both dogs, taking comfort from their warm bodies. Tiggy licked her face, and Scut whined softly.

She felt better then, for a while. But the long walk back gave her time to think, so by the time she reached Conker Road the tears were threatening to spill over again.

Mrs Finnerty answered her frantic banging on Mr Fitzhenry's door. As Felicity shot in with the dogs, Mrs Finnerty said sharply, 'Just a minute, young lady! What do you think you're up to?' Then she saw Felicity's face, and went silent.

'It's nothing, Mrs Finnerty,' Felicity said in a choked voice. 'It's nothing, really .... I'm just being silly.'

'Into the kitchen with you,' Mrs Finnerty commanded. 'There's tea in the pot.'

Mr Fitzhenry was sitting at the kitchen table, finishing his dinner. Mrs Finnerty got out a mug for Felicity and poured her some tea. Then she cut a big slice of fruit cake and put that in front of Felicity too.

'Get that into you, now, and you'll feel better,' she said. 'I'm not one bit surprised to find you wandering around upset, with no mother at home to look after you.'

'She'll be home soon, Mrs Finnerty,' Felicity explained, 'and Mrs Durkin is there now.'

'Does Mrs Durkin feed you?'

'No .... But we can look after ourselves.'

Mrs Finnerty gave a loud 'Hmph!' to signal her

disapproval of working mothers, and went off into the dining-room with a handful of polishing cloths.

Mr Fitzhenry was staring at Felicity. Felicity felt the tears welling up again and gulped a mouthful of scalding tea, hoping it would deaden her desire to cry. But it was no use.

'What's the matter, lassie?'

Mr Fitzhenry's unaccustomed concern undid Felicity completely. She put her head down on the table and bawled.

Mr Fitzhenry, at a loss, kept saying, 'There, there! There, there!' But he let her cry, which was best in the end.

Finally, Felicity was able to tell him what it was all about.

'They're taking our woods, Mr Fitzhenry .... They're taking the Red Belly away from us for some Old People's Home. Oh, Mr Fitzhenry, the Red Belly is the best tree in the whole world .... If only you knew ....' Felicity suddenly found herself telling him everything.

Old Fitzy listened, and when she'd come to a stop he nodded sadly and said, 'Know all about the Home. There's a place reserved for me there. I'll be moving in the spring.'

Felicity gaped at him in astonishment, her tears forgotten. 'But you've got your house. You've got your garden. Why would you want to live in a Home?'

'I don't want to,' said Mr Fitzhenry shortly. 'They tell me there's no other way. I can't look after this place any more. I can't even look after myself. It's for the best.' His face had a tight, hurt expression.

'You don't *look* like you think it's for the best,' Felicity said.

'The dogs ....' Mr Fitzhenry said slowly. 'They don't allow dogs in the Home. They'll have to be put down.'

'You mean *killed*?' Felicity was horrified.

Old Fitzy nodded.

'But you can get them new homes!'

Mr Fitzhenry shook his head. 'Tiggy's been with me too long. She'd never settle with a stranger — and Scut would fret without her. Best to put both of them out of their misery.'

'You can't do that, Mr Fitzhenry, you just *can't*!' Felicity shouted, bringing Mrs Finnerty running in to see what was going on.

Mr Fitzhenry looked distressed.

'Why don't you let me have them?' Felicity suggested frantically. 'I'm not a stranger — I love them and they love me. They're used to me looking after them.'

Mr Fitzhenry said nothing for a long time; he just sat staring at his teacup. When he finally spoke, his voice was barely audible. 'Would your mother agree?'

'Of course she'd agree!' Felicity cried. 'She says we should always try and help people ....' Felicity stopped, suddenly remembering how much Mr Fitzhenry hated being helped.

Then she had the most wonderful idea.

'Mr Fitzhenry, if you let me have Tiggy and Scut, not only would you be helping me, you'd be helping the whole gang.'

Old Fitzy looked up. 'How so?'

'Then I'll have something you want, and, when you go into the Home, you'll have something we want. Don't you see? I can bring Tiggy and Scut to visit you every day, and while you spend time with them, me and the gang can spend time up the Red Belly. We'd be allowed in to the grounds as long as we were visiting you. So you'd be doing us a big favour — and it'd be a fair swop, too.'

Mr Fitzhenry actually smiled. 'Well, lassie, that's quite an offer.'

'So you'll agree?'

'How could I refuse?'

'Oh, Mr Fitzhenry, you're brilliant!' Felicity got up and flung her arms around him in a hug. Mrs Finnerty coughed loudly and busied herself banging dishes around.

Felicity was ecstatic. 'I'll go and tell my mum right now. Thanks, Mr Fitzhenry — oh, thanks!'

☆   ☆   ☆

Felicity ran home, full of excitement, and burst in through the back door. Her mother was sitting at the kitchen table as usual, having a cup of tea.

'Oh, Mum! Mum! I have the most wonderful news! Mr Fitzhenry is giving me Tiggy and Scut to keep —'

Mrs Kelly's face darkened. 'No, Felicity. I said *no!*'

'But, Mum, just let me explain. Mr Fitzhenry is going to the new Old People's Home and they won't allow pets. If I don't take them, Tiggy and Scut will have to be put down.'

'I said no, Felicity. I don't want dogs in the house. You know that very well.'

'But they'll be put to death!'

'Don't be so dramatic, Felicity. Somebody else will give them a home.'

'No — you don't understand. Mr Fitzhenry won't let them go to anybody else. He says they'd only fret.'

'Felicity, we've been through all this before. I've told you time and time again, no dogs ... and I mean it. That's final!' Mrs Kelly turned back to her cup of tea.

Felicity's excitement turned to fury. How could her mother just sit there drinking tea when Tiggy and Scut were going to their deaths? Why was she saying no, when she'd always insisted they should help people? Last year, she'd forced the gang to offer their services to Mr Fitzhenry when they didn't want to. Now, in a dire emergency, she was refusing to help .... Why?

The truth hit Felicity with a sharp, cold shock. Her mother didn't want the bother! Never mind the bother it had caused the gang, spending half the summer slaving in old Fitzy's garden — that was all right; it was somebody else being bothered. But when it involved putting herself out ... that was a different story.

Felicity stared at her mother as if she was seeing her for the first time. The angry words were out before she could stop them.

'You're a *hypocrite*!' she screamed.

Her mother's white, shocked face swam in and out of focus in front of her as the tears came again.

Felicity turned and fled.

She ran out the side gate, into the lane, and down to the woods, jumping over the hateful strip of concrete. In among the trees, she ran and ran and ran until she reached the big, solid trunk of the Red Belly. Up she climbed.

Huddled in the Crow's Nest, she shut her eyes tightly and tried to sort out the teeming thoughts in her head. Everything was going wrong this summer. The world she knew was changing far too fast. Her school was gone — she didn't belong there any more. Soon the woods would be gone too, the Red Belly would be gone, Mr Fitzhenry would be gone from Conker Road, Tiggy and Scut would be gone .... And her mother ... her mother was a hypocrite.

For the first time, Felicity dared to think of that awful word she'd used. She saw again her mother's shocked face. But she felt no remorse. A cold, unfamiliar awareness had settled inside her. Mothers were right, weren't they? Mothers were always right. But this time her mother was wrong — oh, so very wrong!

Felicity realised she'd caught her mother being thoroughly selfish. It was the first time she'd seen any real fault in either of her parents, and her world had

139

shifted on its axis. Never again would she be able to look at things the same way.

She sat up in the Red Belly for hours, unwilling to get down and face this strange new world. Up here in the Crow's Nest it was safe, unchanging.

'Felicity! ... Felicity!'

When the call finally came, Felicity was astonished to discover that it was a quarter past six. She'd been up the Red Belly all afternoon. But her time hadn't been wasted, for she had made up her mind firmly on two things:

First, she would apologise to her mother; and, second, she was taking Mr Fitzhenry's dogs, whether her mother agreed or not — because it was the right thing to do.

Satisfied with her decisions, Felicity climbed down the Red Belly and went home.

☆   ☆   ☆

Mrs Kelly was putting the dinner on the table when Felicity arrived.

After washing her hands quickly, Felicity sat down. Jonathan and her dad were already at the table.

When Mrs Kelly went back out to the kitchen to fetch something, and Mr Kelly got up and went after her, Jonathan took the opportunity to hiss, 'What's going on, Sis? They were in a right flap when I got home.'

Felicity shook her head in warning as their parents came back and sat down.

'Mum ....' she started.

'Felicity ....' Mrs Kelly began, at the same time.

'Mum, I want to say I'm sorry for what I called you earlier on,' Felicity said quickly, silencing her mother, 'but I'm taking Tiggy and Scut whether you like it or not —'

Her mother put up a hand to stop her. 'That's what I

was trying to tell you, Felicity. Your dad and I have had a talk, and we both agree you're right. It's the only decent thing to do.'

'You mean I can have the dogs?' Felicity asked, hardly able to believe what she was hearing.

Her mother nodded, and her father smiled.

'Would somebody tell *me* what's going on?' Jonathan demanded truculently.

'Tell you later,' said Felicity, as she tucked into her dinner.

Just now she was too busy savouring the sweet, incomparable flavour of victory.

The next day, the gang were back in old Fitzy's garden. The others were astonished to hear that Felicity was getting Tiggy and Scut.

'Trust you to wangle it in the end,' Jonathan had said, the previous evening.

'I didn't wangle it!' Felicity had protested. 'It was a matter of life or death.'

'Good story, all the same. How did you think that one up?'

'It's *not* a story,' Felicity had said, outraged. 'It's true.'

'Oh, yeah!'

'Just wait till tomorrow — you can ask old Fitzy yourself.'

And he did. Old Fitzy confirmed Felicity's story to the rest of the gang.

'So you're really moving to the Old People's Home?' Mackey asked.

Mr Fitzhenry nodded.

Mackey suddenly thought of the room full of African masks and carved warriors that they'd discovered in old Fitzy's house the summer before. Mr Fitzhenry had gone out one day, leaving them working in the garden, and they'd sneaked into his house to explore.

Now, as the rest of the gang went to get the gardening tools out of the shed, Mackey hung back.

'How will you have room for all your things in the new place?' he asked casually.

'I won't,' Mr Fitzhenry said. 'Most of them will have to go.'

Mackey was being careful.

'Any old souvenirs, or anything, that you want to get rid of?'

Mr Fitzhenry stared at Mackey long and hard.

'It's OK ... I was just asking,' Mackey gulped, and bolted off to help the others.

'He knows!' he hissed to the rest of the gang. 'He knows about us being in his sitting-room last year.'

'How could he?' Orla protested.

'He knows. You should have seen the way he looked at me when I asked him if he had any old souvenirs.'

'You didn't!' Orla was aghast.

'Well, they're brilliant things, they are,' Mackey said defiantly. 'I wouldn't mind getting a few warriors.'

'Nor me,' said Muggins.

'Remember the African shields?' Jonathan's face lit up. 'They had those weird faces with insects crawling all over them.'

'And the witch doctor's mask — it was deadly too,' Mackey added.

'You nearly got us into awful trouble with that,' Joan sniffed.

Mackey chuckled, remembering how he'd stumbled because he couldn't see properly with the mask over his head and had upset the warriors all over the floor. The gang had been terrified that old Fitzy would come back before they could put the room in order again.

'Come on, Mackey, we've got work to do,' Orla reminded him. 'You can help Jonathan with the lawn.'

The got on with their gardening. Joan had brought Kevin along, as usual, and old Fitzy was kept busy shooing him away from the shore beneath the kitchen window. By twelve o'clock the garden was done, and the gang said goodbye to Mr Fitzhenry for another week.

☆   ☆   ☆

At half past one Mackey was banging on the Kellys' back door.

'There's something funny going on out in the woods,' he said. 'Come and see.'

Jonathan and Felicity abandoned the remains of their lunch and followed Mackey down the lane. They were barely into the woods when Mackey said 'Look!' and pointed at one of the trees.

A big '20' had been marked on the trunk in bright yellow paint.

'Harold!' Jonathan said. 'Harold's messing again.'

'No — look here, too ....' Mackey moved up a bit. The next tree was numbered '19', and the one beyond that '18'. 'They're numbered in a line all the way back to the field. Come and I'll show you.'

They followed Mackey until they reached the tree that was marked '1'. It was on the very edge of the woods.

The field was a tangle of activity.

'They're digging the foundations for the Old People's Home,' Mackey said. 'Must have been at it all morning. They've loads done.'

They stood and stared at the chaos in front of them. Their beloved field was almost unrecognisable.

Felicity sighed. 'So that's it.'

'Maybe not,' said Mackey. 'Suppose the trees are numbered for cutting down?'

'But the Council said they weren't cutting down trees.'

'Precisely.' Mackey grinned.

'I still think Harold put the numbers there,' Jonathan insisted. 'He was probably marking out his territory. After all, we know he has the yellow paint — he used it on the Yellow Belly last year.'

Mackey shook his head. 'Bet it wasn't him.'

'Bet it was.'

'Bet it wasn't.'

'Why don't we just ask him?' Felicity suggested.

'OK, then,' Mackey said. 'But let's get the others first.'

☆   ☆   ☆

They found Harold up the Yellow Belly with his gang.

'Harold! Harold!' Felicity called.

Harold peered over the edge of a branch and surveyed the Red Belly gang with suspicion.

'What do you want?'

'We want to ask you something.'

'What?'

'Did you paint numbers on some of the trees?'

'No.'

Felicity pointed. 'A whole line of trees over there have yellow numbers on them.'

'Well, I didn't do it,' Harold said.

'Did Billy or Mark?'

'No, they didn't! Why do you always blame us for everything?'

'We're not blaming you. We're just checking with you first. There's something fishy going on. Will you come down and look?'

Harold held a huddled consultation with his gang and then said, 'OK, we're coming.'

They swung down the Yellow Belly and joined the Red Belly gang. They all trooped back to the line of marked trees.

Harold stared at the trees with narrowed eyes. 'They're marked for cutting down,' he stated.

'That's what we think too,' said Felicity.

'The County Council have a right cheek!' Joan said.

'We've got them!' Mackey gloated. 'When people hear about this, they won't be allowed to build their wall after all.'

'I could get the photographer back,' Harold offered.

'No, thanks!' Mackey scoffed. 'Fat lot of good it did last time.'

'This is different,' Orla pointed out. 'People didn't care about the woods being taken away from us, but they will care about trees being cut down.'

'He could photograph us up the marked trees,' Harold suggested. 'That would look good — as if we were having a sit-in up there.'

'We're not allowed to have sit-ins any more,' Joan told him. 'There's a court injunction against us.'

'I know,' Harold said, 'but it won't cover this. They never told the court that they were going to cut down trees, did they?'

'No, they didn't,' Mackey grinned. 'They didn't let on to anybody.'

'I'll contact the paper, so,' Harold decided. 'I'm sure they'll be very interested.'

'OK, what do you want in exchange this time?' Jonathan asked, resigned.

Harold put on a hurt expression. 'I don't want anything.'

'I don't believe it!'

'I'm doing it to help you.'

'Yeah? What's the catch?' Mackey demanded.

Harold shrugged. 'Oh, well, if you don't want me to ....'

'Of course we do,' Felicity broke in quickly, with a warning glare at Jonathan and Mackey.

'Right, then,' said Harold, all business now. 'I'll go and make a phone call.'

He took himself off in the direction of the lane, with Billy and Mark trotting after him.

☆   ☆   ☆

In the meantime, the Red Belly gang called to every house on Conker Road. The reaction they got was astounding. Everybody was up in arms at the very mention of trees being cut down. Quite a few people promised to phone the County Council themselves.

The photographer came out to Conker Woods late in the afternoon. Harold had them all organised, up the trees, before he arrived. He and Billy and Mark were joining in the protest this time. The photographer took lots of shots from different angles.

When he'd gone, Jonathan asked, 'When is the reporter coming?'

'He's not,' Harold replied calmly. 'I told the paper the story myself — after all, the reporter didn't tell it very well last time, did he?'

They had to agree that he hadn't.

'Pity the *Village News* isn't out until tomorrow afternoon,' Felicity said, excited. 'I can hardly wait!'

'Why don't we all go to the newsagent's at lunchtime and hang around?' Jonathan suggested. 'Then we'll get the very first copy when it arrives.'

Harold just smiled.

☆   ☆   ☆

The next morning, they found out what Harold had been smiling about.

Their photograph was on the front page of a national newspaper!

Mackey's mum discovered it first, as she had her paper delivered to the house. Mackey came running out to tell the others.

They stared at the picture in consternation.

It was a good one, big and clear. The only thing was that Harold and his gang were in the very front, up tree number 19, while the Red Belly gang were in the background, up the trees numbered 18 and 17.

'You can hardly see us!' Jonathan complained.

'It's a great photograph — of Harold and Billy and Mark!' said Joan.

'They're hogging the whole thing!' Mackey fumed.

Worse was to come.

When Jonathan read the accompanying column, they discovered that Harold was described as the spokesperson for the people of Conker Road. The whole campaign to save Conker Woods, in fact, was attributed to 'Harold Hanley, a civic-minded young man who is a shining example to his community'.

'I don't believe this!' raged Mackey. 'We sit in that lane for two horrible days, and he takes all the credit!'

'Well, he's got us the publicity we wanted,' Orla said. 'Does it really matter who gets the credit?'

'Yes, it does,' Mackey growled, 'if it's Harold.'

☆　　☆　　☆

Things happened quickly after that. Harold was invited to speak on local radio — he made a good job of it, too. The County Council was flooded with calls protesting about the trees being cut down. Local representatives were galvanised into action by the strength of public opinion.

The *Village News* missed the whole story — the reporter they'd sent before came nosing around in the afternoon, but none of the gang would speak to him.

'Serves him right,' Felicity declared. 'He didn't take us seriously last time.'

By Friday morning, it was all over.

A statement from the County Council was published in the national papers. The Council were not going to cut down any trees. They were not going to build any walls. They were not going to interfere with Conker Woods at all. They were going to erect a chain-link fence around the site for the Retirement Home while building was in progress. They would review matters in the spring.

'Hip-hip-hooray! We've won!' Mackey crowed when he read it.

'They've given in completely!' Felicity was astonished.

'And the Red Belly is safe,' Muggins beamed.

'Until spring,' Orla said warningly. 'They'll try again.'

'No they won't!' Mackey declared triumphantly. 'Because if they do, we'll be waiting for them ....'

'Well, I'm glad that's over,' Joan said. 'Now things can get back to normal.'

It was good to be back in the woods, knowing it was theirs again.

The gang held a party up the Red Belly, then climbed to the very top to watch the work in progress on the Retirement Home.

'It won't make much difference to us,' Joan said. 'There's still some of the field left.'

'Wonder what they'll build on that?' Mackey snorted.

'Nobody's building anything on it ... are they?'

'Give them time — they'll fill the whole place with concrete.'

'Well, we've got the woods,' Felicity said, 'and we've got the Red Belly. That's all that matters now.'

Life drifted back to normal.

Orla was at her old tricks again, wanting to go up to the village all the time, but now she pestered the gang to come with her.

'My mum's being a pain — she seems to think someone will run away with me if I'm by myself.'

'Run away *from* you, more likely, with that hair,' Muggins sniggered.

Orla had not only hacked her hair with nail scissors again, but also painted the tips of the resulting spikes with black dye, which looked quite bizarre against her red hair.

Mackey thoroughly approved, running his fingers speculatively through his own dark hair. 'They won't let you into school like that, though, will they?' he asked.

Orla shook her head. 'No. I'll have to cut it all off

again for September. Maybe I'll shave it next time.'

'They won't let you into school like that, either!'

'Probably not. They're a pain. I'll have to settle for it really short all over.' Orla sighed, then perked up again. 'Who's coming to the village with me?'

'I've no money,' Jonathan said.

'Neither have I,' said Orla impatiently. 'We're not going to buy sweets.'

'Then why are we going?'

Felicity giggled at Jonathan's question.

'Just to hang around,' Orla said. 'We don't have to be *doing* anything.'

Jonathan looked confused, but decided not to pursue the matter further.

'I don't want to go,' Joan said flatly.

Orla lost her temper.

'You don't want to go! Do you think I wanted to hang around here this past week? Do you think I wanted to wreck my nails digging, and sit in the pouring rain all night? I did it to support you lot — and did you hear me complain? Now you won't even come to the village with me. Some friends you are!'

They were all taken aback.

Finally, Felicity said, 'OK, Orla, fair point. We'll come with you.'

'Good,' Orla replied — in the sort of voice that meant, 'Big deal!'

They walked to the village and sat on the bench outside the newsagent's shop. Joan had extracted money from her dad; she bought a big bag of toffees and passed them around. They sat in the sunshine, chewing.

'Are you going to visit your granny, Joan?' Felicity asked. Joan's granny lived in the village.

Joan shook her head. 'No. She'll be at college, or else she'll be writing an essay, or doing research. There's no point in going near her during the week. She's bringing me to the pictures on Saturday, anyway.'

'Why does she work in the holidays?'

'She's going to summer school.'

'I miss her rock buns,' Muggins said.

'So do I,' Joan sighed. 'She never has time for baking now.'

'Must be weird for you, not having her in your house any more,' Jonathan said. 'She looked after you for so long.'

'It was at first,' Joan admitted, 'but Granny says we all have to accept changes — nothing stands still.'

'I'm standing still ... look!' Mackey shouted. He'd climbed up on the wall beside the shop and was posing like a statue.

'Get down, Mackey,' Orla said. 'You can be *so* juvenile!'

But Mackey was having fun. 'I spy ... with my little eye ... something in-ter-es-ting! Hey, look at the cut of yer man over there!' He pointed.

Across the road, a youth came into sight. He was very tall and had his hair tied back in a ponytail. He carried a red guitar on a strap slung around his shoulders, but he held the guitar in front, as if he was about to break into music at any minute.

'Show-off!' Mackey shouted. Then, to the gang, he said, 'You'd think he'd put his guitar in a case for carrying, like anybody else.'

Orla had gone very red. 'Shut up, Mackey,' she hissed. 'Shut *up*! And if you don't get down off that wall, I'll strangle you!'

'That's Orla's fella,' Muggins sniggered.

'He's not my fella.' Orla was scarlet. She gave Muggins a hefty thump.

But Muggins wasn't shutting up. 'She comes down here every day to watch for him .... Ouch! Stop it!' Orla was viciously kicking his ankles with her Doc Marten boots.

The youth never even looked their way.

They watched him as he walked down to the other end of the village.

'Red Belly!' Joan giggled. 'We should call him Red Belly ... the way he holds that red guitar across his middle.'

'*Orla's* Red Belly,' Felicity grinned, 'since she's lost interest in the real one.'

'I'm never speaking to you lot again!' Orla got up and stomped off in the direction of home.

'Orla ... wait! We were only joking!' Felicity ran after her. The others followed, wide grins on their faces.

☆   ☆   ☆

The next day they went up to the village again. They wanted to call on Dara's granny. On the way, to appease Orla, they sat outside the newsagent's for a while and waited for the guy with the guitar to go past again.

'He must practise around here somewhere,' Jonathan reckoned.

'I wouldn't mind learning the guitar,' Muggins said enviously.

'Neither would I,' Jonathan admitted.

Orla was quiet, but she never took her eyes off the youth with the red guitar until he disappeared off into the distance. Then she stood up. 'Come on, let's go and see Dara's granny.'

The gang wanted to find out if she knew when Dara was returning from Zambia. He was due to start secondary school with them at the beginning of September, but the gang still hadn't had a letter. His granny told them he was flying in on the last Saturday in August.

'But that won't give him time to get a uniform,' Muggins protested. 'We start school the next week.'

'I've got his uniform already,' Dara's granny told them. 'His mother sent me his measurements.'

So that was that. The gang had been hoping he would come a bit earlier and enjoy at least some of the summer holidays with them.

☆　　☆　　☆

The trip up to the village became a daily routine. They never stayed very long, but the guy with the guitar always went past while they were there. It kept Orla quiet, and she was happy to mess around in the woods with them afterwards.

They still teased her, of course, but she only said huffily, 'I *haven't* got a crush on him — I just think he's nice. He makes a change from looking at you juveniles.'

'I'm not a juvenile,' Mackey protested.

'Nor me.' Jonathan was offended.

'Don't mind her,' Muggins advised them. 'She just likes using that word — it's her favourite at the moment. She calls me juvenile all the time.'

'Oh, grow up, the lot of you!' said Orla, exasperated.

☆　　☆　　☆

The Old People's Home was being erected at an astonishing speed. Some of the walls were quite high already. The whole site had been securely enclosed by ten-foot-high chain-link fencing topped with rolls of barbed wire.

'I wish I could get in there with a big hammer,' growled Mackey.

'You wouldn't do much harm with a hammer,' Jonathan said.

'Well, a JCB, then. If I could get hold of a JCB and knock all those walls down ....'

'Don't be stupid,' Orla said. 'They'd only build them up again. Why don't you stop fighting it and accept that the field is gone?'

Mackey glowered through the fence, but said nothing more.

☆   ☆   ☆

Harold came looking for payment from the Red Belly gang.

Mackey had to spend an afternoon showing him and Billy and Mark how to do parachute rolls. Billy and Mark were quick learners, he discovered. By the end of the afternoon they were jumping out of the Yellow Belly and hitting the ground like true experts.

The rest of the gang sat on the Captain's Table and watched the show. Arnie had to be brought home, as he got upset every time Harold fell out of the tree. Columbus had to be brought home too, for a different reason. He went on a rat-hunt while the training was going on. By the time he'd deposited his third dead rat beneath the Captain's Table, the gang had had enough.

'Get rid of that disgusting dog!' Joan howled.

'Hey, Mackey, it's getting to be a bit much!' Jonathan protested.

'I'm going to be sick,' Muggins wailed.

Mackey took Columbus home and locked him in the shed.

Harold hadn't forgotten about the Tunnel, either.

'You're doing well out of this,' Mackey growled.

'I helped you to save the woods, didn't I?' Harold pointed out.

'And took all the credit, too.'

'I'm not responsible for what the newspaper decides to print. I didn't ask them to say that.'

'Oh, yeah?' Mackey scoffed.

'The Tunnel, if you please,' said Harold calmly. Billy and Mark were staring at him in open admiration.

Harold got his way. The Red Belly gang had promised, so there was no backing out. Mackey was still grumbling, so Felicity and Joan took over and showed the Yellow Bellies their hiding-place.

Billy and Mark were ecstatic — they thought it was the best thing in the whole woods.

Felicity felt a pang at their excitement. She remembered feeling the same way herself, when the Red Belly gang had first found the Tunnel. Now that they were used to it, it didn't seem half as wonderful any more.

The girls left Harold and Billy and Mark in the Tunnel and rejoined the rest of the gang.

'They're a better size for the Tunnel than we are now,' Joan admitted.

'We can still use it too, can't we?' Muggins broke in anxiously.

'Of course we can,' said Felicity quickly.

But they knew they wouldn't.

☆   ☆   ☆

Up the Red Belly, that evening, they pledged that they would always be friends.

So much was changing. Secondary school loomed. It was unknown territory. They might not even be in the same class any more. But they'd be there for one another — no matter what ....

Mackey produced his penknife and insisted that they mingle blood.

'Indian tribes do it,' he said, 'as an initiation into growing up. If we mingle blood, then we'll always be brothers.'

'And sisters,' Joan objected.

'Well, you know what I mean,' Mackey said.

'We'll always belong to the Red Belly,' Felicity declared. 'We're bonded to it forever.'

'Great idea!' said Mackey enthusiastically. 'We'll leave our blood here in the Crow's Nest, too.'

So, one by one, they each carefully cut an index finger with the blade of Mackey's penknife, and the six of them pressed their cut fingers together until they

were sure the blood was properly mingled. Then they each deposited a few drops of blood right in the centre of the Crow's Nest.

'Done!' said Mackey triumphantly.

'What about Dara?' Muggins asked.

There was silence. They'd forgotten about Dara.

'Well, he's not here, is he?' Mackey said defensively. 'He'll just have to do it when he gets home.'

'I'm not slitting my finger again for anyone,' Joan declared. She was pressing hard on her finger, trying to stop the bleeding.

'He can leave his blood in the Crow's Nest with ours — that'll do,' said Mackey.

Afterwards, they climbed to the top of the Red Belly to watch the sunset. It got dark earlier now, at about half past nine. The sun was already low in the sky when they took their places on the topmost branches. With their backs to the field, they couldn't see the awful building scars. Instead, they faced into the setting sun.

Down in the Crow's Nest, it had grown quite dim; but up here, everything was a blaze of brightness. They swayed on their familiar high perches, with the whole of Conker Woods at their feet. Their skin had turned to gold, the branches they clung to had turned to gold, as the brilliant globe of the sun set the Red Belly alight.

'We're golden people, up a golden tree, in a golden land,' said Felicity happily.

They stayed up there, watching, as the sun slipped slowly behind the horizon, until it was gone.

Then Orla said, 'Better get down out of here while we can still see.'

They raced each other down the Red Belly, dropping the last few feet to the ground in perfect parachute rolls; then they slipped like shadows through the darkened woods, towards the lights of home.

Unexpected Happenings

The following Wednesday was hot and sultry, with an airless feel. The gang worked in Mr Fitzhenry's garden as best they could. They cut the grass and did a bit of weeding. The garden was in pretty good shape now, so it was easy to keep tidy. But they were strangely restless and lacking in energy for this sort of thing.

Old Fitzy was restless too. He paced up and down the path by the back door. Several times they caught him leaning on his walking-stick, just staring at them.

'What's up with him today?' Mackey complained. 'He's got a right bee in his bonnet.'

'He misses Kevin,' said Felicity.

'Kevin was so cross this morning I had to leave him at home,' Joan sighed.

Orla was sitting on the grass, fanning herself with a big leaf. 'It's so hot .... I wouldn't mind, but there isn't even any sun.' She glanced up at the overcast sky, then down to where Tiggy and Scut and Columbus were asleep in the shade of the big hedge. 'Look at those dogs — they're usually running around like mad things!'

Mrs Finnerty brought the gang out cold drinks and biscuits at half past ten, which made them feel a bit cooler. But by twelve o'clock they'd had enough. They packed the tools away in the garden shed.

Old Fitzy was waiting for them by the back door. 'I've something to show you,' he said.

He turned and went into the house. The gang followed.

Mr Fitzhenry clumped up the hall and opened the sitting-room door. He stood back and motioned to them to go in.

The room was exactly as they remembered it.

African masks lined the walls in a riot of colour — fantastic faces with long chins, insects carved all over them. On the floor, an army of fierce ebony warriors stood ready for battle, clutching shields and hatchets and spears. Woven rugs draped the sofas. A large crocodile occupied the mantelpiece, tail hanging over the edge. Everything was covered in dust.

The gang stared, silently absorbing the scene.

In front of them, on the wall, was the photograph they'd wondered about before — a young man carrying a rifle, with a dead lion at his feet. He had one foot propped up on the lion's body.

'Is that you, Mr Fitzhenry?' Jonathan asked.

Mr Fitzhenry nodded.

'But you're not allowed to shoot lions any more, are you?' Felicity enquired anxiously.

'No,' Mr Fitzhenry said. 'That was in the past. We didn't know any better then.'

'That's 'cause you didn't have Greenpeace,' Mackey declared.

'I don't think it's Greenpeace.' Old Fitzy was smiling. 'It's just changing times.'

'But it's better now, isn't it?'

'Some things ....' Mr Fitzhenry looked around the room, and for a minute said nothing more. Then he waved a hand at all the African stuff. 'You can have this if you like. Divide it up between you. I won't be able to bring it with me to the Retirement Home.'

'D'ya really mean that?' Mackey gasped. 'Can we have it today?'

Felicity glanced at Mr Fitzhenry. He was losing so much — had so many changes to adjust to .... 'No, we can't,' she said quickly, with a warning frown at Mackey. 'We can have it in the spring, when Mr Fitzhenry is ready to move.'

There was relief on old Fitzy's face. 'Yes,' he agreed, 'in the spring.'

'Are you not keeping any for yourself?' Muggins asked.

'A few pieces. That's all I'll have room for.'

'And we can really have the rest?'

Old Fitzy nodded.

'It's the best present I've ever got in my whole life!' Muggins declared.

'And mine,' said Mackey, 'after Columbus, of course.'

Mr Fitzhenry looked pleased.

Orla was fingering one of the masks with delight. 'Oh, Mr Fitzhenry, it'll make my bedroom dead interesting. It's so-o-o boring at the moment.'

Jonathan and Joan were trying to count the warriors, but it was an impossible task — there were warriors behind armchairs and sofas and other things, as well as in the middle of the floor.

'Thanks, Mr Fitzhenry,' Felicity said. 'It's brilliant of you to offer the things to us. But if you ever change your mind and want them back, that'll be OK.'

Mrs Finnerty was out in the hall, brandishing a feather duster. She glared through the doorway. 'Dust-catchers!' she said scathingly. 'He won't let me near them.'

Mr Fitzhenry quickly ushered the gang out of the room again and closed the door. He and Mrs Finnerty stood eye to eye for a moment before Mrs Finnerty gave a loud 'Hmph!' and went bustling up the stairs.

Old Fitzy let them out the front door, holding it open while Mackey went back to call Columbus and Felicity fetched Tiggy and Scut to bring them for their walk.

☆　　☆　　☆

Throughout that afternoon, the sky grew darker and darker. By four o'clock it was like dusk. The weather was hot and oppressive, so that the gang still felt restless, no matter what they tried to do. A strong wind had blown up, but it was a hot wind, and the trees in Conker Woods tossed and swayed, restless too.

The gang stayed out in the woods, even when the first heavy drops of rain became a torrential downpour. It took a heavy clap of thunder to send them scurrying homewards.

'Being out in the rain is really dangerous in a thunderstorm,' Orla warned them. As if to reinforce her words, there was a bright flash of lightning in the distance, then another clap of thunder.

'Come back to my place,' Joan shouted. 'My dad won't mind.'

Mr O'Brien was lying on the sofa in the sitting-room, watching television. Kevin was happily playing with his toys on the floor. As the next flash of lightning made the television picture turn to snow, Mr O'Brien switched it off, then got up and unplugged the set.

'Don't turn on any lights till the storm passes,' he told the gang.

It was quite dark in the house now, but they went into the dining-room and decided to try to play Scrabble. Joan got out the Scrabble board and set it up on the dining-room table. They started to play, keeping one eye warily on the storm outside.

The rain pounded against the window as the wind changed, and for a moment they couldn't even see out. Then the wind swung around again and a bright flash of lightning zigzagged across the sky.

'Forked lightning!' Mackey said. 'That's really dangerous. It can come down the chimney after you — fella in the pub told me some stories ....'

But Muggins didn't want to hear any more. With a

whimper of fear he was underneath the table, his T-shirt pulled over his head. The others laughed — until a clap of thunder came, so loud that it rattled the house.

They all joined Muggins under the table.

Mackey tried to continue with his stories, but Joan shrieked at him to stop. The next sharp crack of lightning silenced him anyway; it silenced them all.

It was awesome. It shot its tentacles across the sky, and the clap of thunder came almost immediately. It was like something heavy falling on the roof of the house. They could feel the vibrations going through the floor beneath them.

'The storm is right overhead,' whispered Joan.

The next flash came straight down, a fork of dazzling brightness. For an instant, the highest point of Conker Woods was lit by an eerie blue light, almost like a halo.

Felicity screamed and screamed. 'The Red Belly! It's been hit! The Red Belly's been hit by lightning!'

A massive crash of thunder drowned out her cries, but she was already out from under the table and dashing to the window, frantically trying to see out. The rain beat straight onto the window as the wind swung around, and Felicity could see nothing in spite of rubbing at the glass.

Then the wind veered away again, and everything was suddenly clear.

'It's still there, stupid!' came Jonathan's voice from under the table. 'What on earth were you screeching about?' He sounded angry — the sort of anger that comes with relief after a fright.

'But I saw ....' Felicity began. 'I saw it being hit ... I'm certain!'

The next flash of lightning came from slightly further away. The rest of the gang waited for the crash of thunder before climbing out from underneath the table to join Felicity at the window.

They stared at the Red Belly, dominating the skyline as always.

Felicity felt limp with relief. For one awful moment she'd thought — really thought — that the Red Belly was gone.

Another flash lit up the sky, and Mackey started counting seconds. 'One ... two ... three ... four ... five. It's a mile away now,' he announced.

They all relaxed.

'That was some joke you played on us,' Mackey said to Felicity.

'It wasn't a joke. I'm certain I saw the Red Belly being hit.'

Joan's dad came in, carrying Kevin. 'Proper scary stuff, that,' he said casually. 'I heard you all having a great scream. Better than a horror movie, wasn't it?'

'No, it wasn't, Dad!' said Joan crossly. 'You're meant to be looking after us. We were really frightened.'

Mr O'Brien chuckled. 'A good fright never did anyone any harm. This chappie wasn't afraid at all.' He put Kevin on the ground, and the child toddled over to Mackey.

'Hi, little fella,' Mackey said. He swung Kevin up onto his shoulders and turned back to the window to show him the flashes of lightning in the distance.

The rain had stopped and everything was suddenly calm. But the sky remained dark.

'You kids had better skedaddle off home while you have the chance,' Mr O'Brien said. 'I don't think we're finished with that storm at all.'

☆　　☆　　☆

That night, Felicity lay in bed and listened to the wind howling around the house. It rose and fell, rose and fell, in blasts of incredible force. Every few minutes something or other — a can, a lid — went clattering away into the night. Once there was a heavy crash on the roof and a smashing sound out back. Felicity dived beneath the covers. She thought the chimney was coming down.

She tossed and turned for ages in the bed, sure she would be awake all night. But gradually the rising and falling of the wind had its own hypnotic effect, and Felicity drifted off into an uneasy sleep.

Then it was morning, and the room was flooded with a pale light.

Felicity opened her eyes and listened. Everything outside was still and quiet. But there was something strange about the quality of the light ... something different. Felicity lay staring out the window, sleepily trying to figure it out. There was too much light — too much sky ....

Her heart gave a sickening lurch as the realisation seeped in. Then she was out of bed, and clinging to the windowsill as she took in the scene outside.

The Red Belly lay with its great head in Conker Lane, the topmost branches just brushing Joan's back gate. Behind it, a long channel had been gouged out of the woods. Felicity's fingers dug into the sill as a terrible scream built up inside her — a scream that wouldn't even come out. No! *Nooo!* This couldn't be happening .... Not the Red Belly!

Quickly she threw on her tracksuit and a pair of trainers and slipped out of the bedroom. Everyone else in the house was still asleep. Felicity let herself quietly out the back door and, shutting her eyes, moved blindly towards the gate. She paced to the end of Conker Lane, feeling her way by the hedge. She knew this was a horrible dream. If she kept her eyes closed until she reached the back lane, then she would open them and find that everything was as normal.

She eased herself around the corner at the bottom of the lane, then stood for a moment, heart pounding, before daring to open her eyes.

It was not a horrible dream. It was a hundred times worse.

The back lane was filled with branches, those same branches that the gang had so often clung to as they reached for the sky. Felicity scrambled in among them, tried to cling to them as before, but they just bent, depositing her gently on the ground again.

She climbed along the tree, looking for the Crow's Nest. Maybe she could rescue their things. But the Crow's Nest was empty — no letters, no wrestling magazines, no survival rations — not even the copper tube that held the map of their Journey to the Centre of the Earth. Felicity scrabbled frantically in the tangles of broken branches beneath the Crow's Nest, but she found nothing. Nothing at all.

She climbed further in, onto the Red Belly's trunk. The splash of red paint was clearly visible on one side. Ahead, the roots of the tree spiralled into the air.

Felicity jumped down, and stood staring at the massive crater in the ground. She turned back again to finger the familiar circle of red paint.

Suddenly, it all became too much to bear. She beat her fists angrily against the Red Belly's enormous bulk.

'Get up, Red Belly! Get up!' she screamed.

Then she threw her arms around the trunk and sobbed as if her world had come to an end. Her cheek was against the rough bark. She pressed it harder, willing the tree to show some sign of life. But there was none. A pool of water formed beneath her face, making her cheek wet and sticky. Her tears ran down the trunk, catching in the crevices of the bark and being absorbed.

Felicity mourned as she'd never mourned over anything — not even over Mackey's dog, Boozer, the year before. The Red Belly had been part of her life for so

long, for as long as she could remember. As a tiny child, like Kevin, she'd watched it from the windows .... Then there had been all those years of longing to climb it .... Now, just when the Red Belly was truly hers at last, it was gone. She'd never climb it again. Never. Never.

A fresh flood of tears came and she cried and cried, sobbing until she was thoroughly exhausted and could cry no longer. But still she clutched the trunk, not wanting to let go — not ever wanting to let go ....

Felicity felt a lick on the back of her neck. She turned around. Columbus covered her face with wet slobbers.

'Cut it out, you pesky dog!' said Mackey, pulling Columbus away.

Columbus went off to explore the Red Belly's crater. Mackey stood there, with his hands in his pockets, watching Felicity carefully.

'You OK?' he asked gruffly.

Felicity's face was hot and puffy from crying, and her throat was raw. She wanted to bawl again, but she had no tears left. 'I don't know,' she said.

Mackey kicked idly at the Red Belly's trunk. He seemed just the same as usual — certainly not upset like Felicity was. She felt a surge of anger.

'How can you be so ... so *normal*?' she burst out. 'Don't you *care* about the Red Belly?'

Mackey's face set into a defensive mask.

'Course I do,' he said, 'but nothing lasts, does it?'

Felicity crouched on the ground, with her back against the fallen tree, and glared at Mackey through swollen eyelids. 'That's a terrible thing to say,' she said fiercely.

Mackey shrugged. 'Well, it's true, isn't it? My baby sister died. My ma and da broke up. Boozer died. Now the Red Belly's gone ....'

Felicity was appalled.

Mackey had known so much loss in his life, so

much real loss — and here she was, crying over a tree. But it didn't feel like just a tree. It felt as if someone close and dear to her had died. The pain of the loss was unlike anything she'd ever experienced before. Suddenly she realised just what Mackey had been going through all this time.

Mackey sat down beside her.

Columbus was busy digging in the crater, sending soil flying up into the air.

'Mackey,' Felicity began carefully, 'when Boozer died, did you feel like this?'

'Like what?'

'Like there was a big empty hole inside you and you wanted to crawl into it and die too?'

Mackey was quiet for a moment. Then he said, very softly, 'Yeah. I felt like that.'

They sat in silence until Columbus decided he'd had enough of digging. With a last kick of his hind legs, he abandoned the Red Belly's crater and padded over to them. He jumped onto Mackey's lap and covered his face with licks.

Mackey put his arms around Columbus. 'Pesky dog!' he laughed. 'Stoppit, will you!'

Columbus finally settled down on the ground, with his head and paws on Mackey's knees.

But Felicity had been thinking about what Mackey had said — that nothing lasts. If that was true — if that was what the future held, if a whole world of un-imaginable losses lay ahead — how could she ever face it? Suddenly she was afraid.

'Mackey ....' She searched his face anxiously. 'Is it really true, what you were saying before?'

'Is what true?'

'That nothing lasts.'

Mackey gave a great sigh. 'Well ... things change. But I suppose ... other things come,' he said grudgingly.

'My sister died, but Joan said Kevin could be my brother. My ma and da split up, but they're still there for me, and now I have two homes. And Boozer died, but then I got Columbus. I don't know about the Red Belly yet.'

Felicity felt a sense of relief. It wasn't all bad, then — and Mackey had somehow coped. Surely she should be able to do the same?

'Do you think your mum and dad will ever get back together?'

Mackey took a couple of minutes to answer this one. 'No,' he said shortly. 'They're going to court for a divorce. My da has a new girlfriend.'

'Oh, Mackey! I'm sorry. Does that mean you might have a stepmother?'

'Yeah ... I might.'

'Does your mum have a boyfriend?'

'No, she doesn't!' Mackey said fiercely. 'Hasn't she got me?'

Felicity decided not to ask any further.

They sat together in companionable silence, with the ruins of the Red Belly all around them. The sky above the clearing was a circle of clear blue. Light flooded into places that hadn't seen the light in years. The clearing felt naked without the canopy of the Red Belly to protect it. The midday sun would scorch the woodland floor.

Columbus had fallen asleep. He sighed deeply — a long, peaceful sigh.

'Lucky Columbus,' thought Felicity, sighing deeply too.

Later that morning, the gang gathered around the Red Belly.

'Look at the size of it!' Jonathan exclaimed. 'It seems even bigger on the ground than it did in the sky.'

'How can a huge tree like that just fall?' Muggins demanded.

'It was hit by lightning,' Felicity insisted. 'I told you it was. I saw it all lit up.'

'There aren't any scorch-marks,' Jonathan pointed out.

'Maybe the lightning just ran down the tree and weakened its roots.'

'My dad says the wind was hurricane-force last night,' said Orla.

'I know,' Jonathan answered. 'It blew a tile off our roof. You should have heard the noise — crash, bang, smaaash!'

'I'm not surprised the Red Belly fell down, with all the holes that Columbus has been digging around it lately,' Joan declared.

'Hey, hold on! You're not going to blame *Columbus*!' Mackey was irate.

'Well, you have to admit it didn't help.'

'He's only a puppy. You leave him out of this — right?' Mackey glared at her. Joan just shrugged.

'Lucky you didn't bury Boozer under the Red Belly, like you wanted to,' Muggins observed. 'He'd be all over the place now.'

'Shut *up*, Muggins!' Orla hissed.

'I was only saying —'

'Let's look for our things from the Crow's Nest,' Jonathan suggested quickly.

'I've searched already. I couldn't find anything,' Felicity said. 'Not a single thing.'

'We'll look again. We'll all look. Come on!'

Jonathan and Muggins and Joan and Mackey went scrambling in among the branches. Columbus burrowed after them, getting under their feet and tripping them up with his enthusiasm.

Felicity and Orla skirted the Red Belly and went into the woods to look at the crater left by the roots. Orla couldn't get over the size of it.

'It's absolutely *huge*! You could build a swimming pool there.' She turned and ran her fingers along the trunk. 'Poor Red Belly,' she said regretfully.

'Poor us,' Felicity retorted.

Columbus came shooting out from under the tree and half-fell, half-slithered into the crater. He started to dig, sending the soil flying in all directions. The others were squealing and laughing as they rooted around in the tangle of branches.

'How can they be so cheerful?' Felicity thought furiously.

There was a sudden commotion in the crater. Two bodies rolled around, locked together; then Arnie made a rapid exit, limping. He stood a safe distance away as Columbus, growling, defended his territory. Harold appeared, with his gang, and quickly knelt down to examine Arnie and make sure he was all right.

Billy and Mark had jumped up onto the Red Belly's trunk and were swinging off one of the overhead roots. 'Hey, look at this. It's brilliant!' they shouted.

'Get out of there! That's our tree,' Felicity said angrily.

'It's not anybody's tree now. It's dead,' Billy shouted back.

'The Council are coming to saw it up into little

pieces,' Mark said. 'We can each have a bit as a souvenir.'

'Hey, that's a great idea!' Jonathan had emerged from the branches with Mackey, and they walked along the trunk towards Billy and Mark.

Felicity couldn't believe her ears. 'You *dare* to bring bits of the Red Belly home, Jonathan Kelly, and I'll never speak to you again!' she yelled at him.

Jonathan looked astonished. 'What's up with her, then?' he said to Mackey.

Joan and Muggins came out along the trunk, shrieking with laughter as they tried to push each other off.

Felicity turned to go. It was all too much. Here they were, laughing and shouting and having fun — and nobody seemed to actually *care* that the Red Belly was gone. She hurried out of the clearing, back into the woods, and headed for Conker Lane.

A voice called from behind her. 'Felicity! Wait for me!' It was Orla. When she caught up with Felicity, she said, 'You're going somewhere fast.'

'I'm not going anywhere,' Felicity fumed. 'I'm just getting away from that jolly lot.' She tossed her head back in the direction they'd come from.

Orla studied her for a moment before saying, 'They're not doing any harm, you know.'

'They don't care. Nobody cares.'

'They do care. It's just their way of dealing with it.'

When Felicity didn't reply, Orla asked, 'Want to come up the village with me, then?'

Felicity nodded. Why not? She certainly didn't want to stay here.

☆   ☆   ☆

That afternoon, a team of council workers arrived with chain-saws. Felicity, unable to bear the sound of the saws, took Tiggy and Scut for a long walk — a very long walk.

When she got back, the council workers had finished for the day. The lane had been cleared, and the timber had been taken away in a lorry. Only Muggins was still hanging around.

'They'll be back tomorrow to do the rest,' Muggins informed her. 'Hope they'll let us into the woods to watch — it's dead exciting ... zzzzz, zzzzz ....' Muggins pretended he was holding a chain-saw and sawing down his back gate. Carly and Shane, who had been clinging to the top of the gate, ran squealing up the garden.

'It's going to be weird without the Red Belly,' Felicity said.

Muggins's arms dropped to his sides, and all the excitement drained out of his face. Suddenly he looked as miserable as Felicity felt.

'I know,' he said. 'Really, really weird.'

☆   ☆   ☆

The next morning, the council workers were back on the job before nine o'clock.

Felicity stayed in bed.

She had a row with Scrub-Scrub at half past eight, when Mrs Durkin discovered her bedroom door locked.

'Go away!' Felicity shouted.

'You let me in there, young lady. I have to clean your room.'

'I'm not getting up today, so there!'

Scrub-Scrub continued to rattle the door handle and bang on the door. Felicity pulled the bedclothes over her head and tried to ignore her. It was a battle of wills, and Felicity won. Eventually Mrs Durkin stomped off, muttering loudly.

By then Felicity was wide awake.

Her bedroom curtains were tightly drawn. No way

did she want to catch a glimpse of what was going on outside. The chain-saws whined and whined like a swarm of gigantic wasps. Felicity switched on her radio to try and drown the noise.

After a while, she got out of bed and started to re-arrange the furniture.

Her bed had always been opposite the window, so that the Red Belly would be in full view. Now she pulled it into a corner, facing a blank wall. Her wardrobe and dressing-table had to be shifted to new positions ....

Scrub-Scrub was banging on the door again, irate.

'I'm just rearranging my room,' Felicity shouted, turning down the radio so she could be heard.

'Makes work for me, that does,' Mrs Durkin complained. 'Moving furniture leaves marks — uncovers dust ....'

'I'll do it, Mrs Durkin,' Felicity shouted back. 'I'll clean my room from top to bottom when I'm finished.' She turned up the radio again, silencing any further arguments.

It wasn't so easy to silence her mother when she came home, at a quarter to two. Mrs Kelly insisted that Felicity open the door.

'You can't stay in your bedroom all day,' she scolded, flicking apart the bedroom curtains and opening the window.

'Why not?' Felicity asked sullenly.

Mrs Kelly surveyed her daughter, her face softening as the whine of the saws outside grew to a crescendo.

'You can't hide away from things,' she said gently. 'You've got to get out there and face them.'

'I was going to,' Felicity said, 'when I was ready.'

Her mother insisted on her eating lunch, even though she wasn't a bit hungry. After her forced feeding, Felicity went up to old Fitzy's and collected Tiggy and Scut for their walk. She stayed out all afternoon.

When she returned, at six o'clock, she found Mackey sitting on the edge of the pavement outside Mr Fitzhenry's house, waiting for her.

'I want to show you something,' he said.

'Be with you in a few minutes,' Felicity promised.

She knocked on Mr Fitzhenry's door. When he opened it, she brought the dogs through to the back garden and quickly filled their bowls with water. Old Fitzy watched her approvingly. She left Tiggy and Scut lapping thirstily.

'Bye, Mr Fitzhenry. See you tomorrow,' Felicity called, letting herself out to rejoin Mackey on Conker Road.

'What is it?' she asked.

'Come and see.'

Mackey led the way down Conker Lane and around the corner towards his back gate. Felicity stopped when she came to the huge gash in the woods.

The Red Belly was gone. Where it had lain, there was a wide path through the trees, littered with saw-dust and bits of twigs and branches.

'Are you coming?' Mackey was impatient.

Felicity followed him into his garden. Mackey pointed, watching her face.

On the ground beneath the cherry tree was a huge slice of the Red Belly's trunk — a massive circle with red paint on one side.

'It's for Boozer,' Mackey explained. 'Now he's buried under the Red Belly, like I always wanted — and it'll stop Columbus digging, too. You don't mind, do you?' He looked at her anxiously.

Felicity smiled, for the first time since the Red Belly had come down, and shook her head. 'For Boozer, no. It's a lovely idea, Mackey.'

Mackey seemed relieved.

'How on earth did you get it here? It must weigh a ton.'

'The council workers did it for me when I explained. Their lorry had a crane attached. They were real nice about it, too.'

Mackey sat down on the huge circle of wood, and Felicity sat beside him.

'There's plenty of room for all of us,' Mackey said. 'Maybe we can sit here sometimes. Then it'll be like Boozer is still included.'

'You could carve his name in the wood.'

'Yeah, I could, couldn't I?'

A call from the direction of the Kellys' house reminded Felicity that she was long overdue for dinner.

Mackey took out his penknife. Felicity left him there, carefully cutting Boozer's name into the very heart of the Red Belly so that the giant growth rings would form a protective frame around it. Mackey, intent on his task, never even noticed that she was gone.

A New Beginning

The first week in September came, and it was time to go back to school.

The Red Belly gang were all going to Conker Hill Secondary School, which was in the village. On the first morning they walked there together, stopping on the way to collect Dara, who had flown back from Zambia the previous Saturday. Dara's granny had held a welcome-home party for him on Sunday, so he hadn't been near Conker Woods yet, although he knew that the Red Belly was gone.

As the gang walked in through the big iron gates of Conker Hill, Mackey was complaining bitterly. Harold's mother had just issued a final warning to Mrs McCarthy: if something wasn't done about Columbus's aggressive behaviour, it would become a matter for the police.

'So now I've to bring him to dog-training classes every Saturday!' Mackey made it sound like a form of torture.

'About time, too,' said Joan. 'You know he needs it.'

'Hey, that's great!' Muggins exclaimed. 'He'll end up like one of those sheepdogs on telly — you'll be able to whistle a command from half a mile away, and he'll obey it.'

Mackey, getting no sympathy from the others on this one, changed the subject. He started to pull at his school uniform.

'Poxy jumper .... You'd think they'd let us wear sweatshirts!'

'At least we don't have to worry about what to put on when we get up in the morning,' Joan pointed out.

'Nothing fits me properly,' Mackey said. 'My ma bought everything to fit me in about five years' time!'

'Tell me about it!' Orla sighed. 'See the length of my skirt? I tried rolling the waistband up, but that just makes me look fat.'

Mackey was staring at Orla. 'Will they let you in with that haircut?'

Orla had been packed off to the hairdresser's the previous week, to have something done about her ragged hair. The hairdresser had been unable to do anything except cut it very short, and Orla had practically no hair left at all.

'They'll have to, won't they?' Orla grinned, fingering her scalp with satisfaction.

Mackey fingered his mop of black hair. 'If they don't expel you, I might get mine done the same way.'

'If your mum lets you!' taunted Joan.

'What's my ma got to do with it?' Mackey snarled. 'I can decide for myself.'

Before this could escalate into a row, Jonathan asked quickly, 'Are you coming back to see the woods this afternoon, Dara?' They only had to attend school for the morning, to meet all their teachers and get their class schedules. The next day, school would start in earnest.

'Of course I am,' Dara said. 'I can't wait!'

'Everything's changed,' Felicity warned him.

'I know, you've told me — but the woods is still there, isn't it?'

Felicity was silent. How could she explain that without the Red Belly, with the concrete strip scarring the lane and the constant noise of the building work in the field beyond, it was just no use any more? Dara would have to find out for himself.

☆   ☆   ☆

They walked home together at lunch-time. Dara left his school-bag at his granny's and told her he would have something to eat with Jonathan and Felicity.

The class allocations hadn't exactly pleased everyone. Felicity and Mackey were together, so were Orla and Jonathan, and Muggins was with Dara, but Joan had ended up on her own and was grumbling about it.

'Why don't you ask your class tutor if you can move in with us?' Felicity asked.

Joan made a face. 'I already did — and got a big lecture on the importance of making new friends!'

'Well, it's not as if we're sitting together in class anyway,' Felicity consoled her. 'Mackey and me were separated. They made everybody move away from people they knew already. Mackey's sitting beside this girl who fancies him!'

'She does not!' Mackey growled. 'She just wouldn't stop looking at me. I had to ask her what she was gawking at.'

But it was Muggins who had picked up the most interesting piece of news. 'Orla's dreamboat is here, in this school!' he announced gleefully.

Orla went very red. 'Shut up, Muggins! You're such a pain!' But when nobody else sought more information, she was forced to ask, very casually, 'How do you know, anyway?'

'I saw him.' Muggins grinned triumphantly. 'And I found out more, too ....'

'What?'

'You told me to shut up.'

Orla gritted her teeth. 'OK, Muggins, I'm sorry. Get on with it, will you!'

Muggins was bursting proudly with his information. 'He's in sixth year — he's a prefect, and he runs the school rock group. They call themselves The Villagers.'

'Poxy name,' Mackey said.

Muggins ignored him. 'And they're allowed to practise in the school hall, even during the holidays. The headmaster thinks they're brilliant.'

'So that's why he was always passing through the village with his guitar,' Felicity said.

'And I found out something else.' Muggins was enjoying the attention. 'He's called Hunk.'

'*Hunk*! That's not his real name, surely?' Joan said, laughing.

'No. He's really Paul Something-or-other, but everybody calls him Hunk.'

'Suits him,' Joan giggled.

Orla said nothing, but she was looking decidedly pleased with Muggins's news.

☆　　☆　　☆

After lunch, they all met in the lane. Columbus ran in circles around Dara, yapping crazily. Dara couldn't get over how big he had grown.

'He's a year old now,' Mackey said proudly, as Dara watched the dog admiringly.

Into the woods they went, to show Dara all the changes.

He stood disconsolately in the Red Belly clearing, surveying the mess. Only the crater remained. Nobody had bothered to fill it in.

'We still have the trees around it,' Dara said, but in a half-hearted sort of way. Noise from the building site filled the woods. 'Let's have a look at the field, then.'

They tramped through the trees until they came to the high chain-link fence that the Council had erected. Noses against the wire, they took in the extent of the work.

'It's huge!' Dara whistled. 'I didn't know it was going

to be that big. How many old people are there, anyway? That'll fit hundreds!'

'Old Fitzy says it's going to be nice. He'll have his own room and everything,' Felicity said.

'I should hope so!' said Joan.

'Well, he says that in other Homes they often have to share,' Felicity explained.

'You mean, sleep in a room with someone you don't even know?'

'Yes.'

'How *awful!*' Joan was horrified.

'Can't imagine sharing a room with old Fitzy,' Dara sniggered.

'Old Fitzy's all right,' Mackey said. 'He's giving us his African stuff.'

'But I gave you African stuff!' Dara looked slightly put out. He'd brought home presents for all of them.

'We're not getting old Fitzy's things until the spring,' Orla explained, 'so we'll have yours in the meantime.'

Dara was somewhat reassured.

They went back to the Red Belly clearing, where Columbus started digging in the crater as usual, sending earth flying up into their faces.

'Shoo! Shoo!' shouted Joan, throwing a twig at him.

Columbus bounded out of the crater and disappeared into the woods, where he started scratching and digging again. They could hear him at it.

'Pesky dog!' Mackey muttered. 'Must've been born down a tunnel.'

'Is he always like this?' Dara asked, laughing.

At that moment, Columbus reappeared, carrying something dirty in his mouth.

'Hey! It's my wrestling magazine,' Mackey cried. 'Where did you find that? Good boy! Give it here.'

Columbus, however, wasn't handing over his treasure. He dodged around Mackey and was gone, tearing into the woods again so fast that nobody had a chance to grab him.

'Something fell out of the magazine,' Joan shouted, running to the edge of the clearing. She bent down and picked it up, then held it triumphantly in the air for the others to see.

It was a small piece of copper piping.

'It's our Journey to the Centre of the Earth!' screeched Muggins.

The year before, they had followed a river to its source and made a fantastic map of their travels — Muggins had done most of it. Joan gave the copper tube to Muggins, who quickly prised out the plasticine plug. He held the tube upside down and shook it. Dark flakes of something floated to the ground.

The gang stared, not understanding, until Felicity exclaimed, 'I told you so! I told you the Red Belly was hit by lightning. Our map is burnt to ashes — that proves I was right.'

'Maybe it just rotted,' Joan said doubtfully.

'It couldn't, not the way it was sealed.'

'Well, it doesn't matter much now, anyway, does it?'

'It'd be nice to have *something* left,' Jonathan grumbled.

They were interrupted by the arrival of Harold, with Arnie in tow. He stood staring at the Red Belly's crater.

'Come to gloat, have you?' Mackey said.

'No, I have not,' Harold replied. 'As a matter of fact, I've come to make you an offer.'

'What kind of an offer?'

'You can use the Yellow Belly if you like. We could share it.'

'Share it!' Mackey scoffed. 'There's hardly enough room up there for you lot, never mind us.'

'You could use it when we're not there.'

'No, thanks!'

'I'm only trying to help.' Harold was hurt.

'It's really nice of you to offer, Harold,' Felicity said gently, 'but I don't think it would work. Thanks all the same.'

There was a sudden commotion in the woods nearby — a loud snarling and yelping. Harold suddenly realised that Arnie had vanished. 'Arnie! Arnie! Come here!' he called.

Mackey moved quickly in the direction of the fighting. He pushed his way through some thick bushes and disappeared. The next minute, Arnie came shooting out into the clearing and ran straight to Harold, who fussed over him anxiously.

Mackey reappeared, holding something in his hands. It was so covered with muck that it took the gang a few seconds to realise what it was.

'Our logbook!' Felicity exclaimed.

'And our survival rations,' Mackey said, holding up a smaller package. 'Columbus had them buried over there in the bushes.'

'No wonder we couldn't find the stuff,' Jonathan spluttered.

'He must have recognised our smell off them,' said Muggins.

Columbus had come out to join them, none too happy at having his cache raided.

'Pesky dog!' Mackey said fondly, giving Columbus a hug. 'You were minding them for us, weren't you?'

The logbook was still in its plastic bag. Mackey opened it and took the book out. It was a bit chewed on one side, and it was glued together with dampness where the rain had got in. He offered it to Felicity. She shook her head and put her hands behind her back as if she was afraid of being forced to take it.

'I'll have it.' Jonathan grabbed the logbook. 'After all, I did most of the writing.'

'It should dry out OK,' Mackey said. 'You can still

185

go on with it; there's plenty of room.'

'There's nothing more to be said!' Felicity declared fiercely. 'It's finished ... *finished*!'

But Felicity was wrong. The final chapter had yet to be written.

TROUBLE

The gang soon settled into the school routine — all except Joan, who was jittery: her dad was due to go back to sea again, and her mother was starting her own career break.

'Imagine, I'll have my mum at home every day!' Joan was all excited. 'It'll be brilliant!'

'That's what you said when your dad was starting *his* career break,' Orla pointed out, laughing.

'I know .... But it'll be really different with my mum,' Joan insisted.

Now that they were coming home so late and the winter evenings were drawing in, they saw little of the woods. Other interests took over. Most of the gang put their names down for the school football teams — Felicity somewhat optimistically, as she didn't really think she'd be any good.

'I'm not good either,' Muggins said, 'but I like playing.'

At the football trials to split everyone up into teams, Joan and Jonathan were picked out and co-opted onto the school athletics team as well. Training took up a good deal of their spare time, but it was fun. Felicity still had to find time to walk the dogs, and the gang gave Mr Fitzhenry's garden a quick tidy most Saturday mornings — just for half an hour, though, or sometimes less.

Orla didn't bother with the football. 'It's so rough,' she complained. 'What if I broke a leg and couldn't do my ballet any more? I'd just die!'

'Drama queen!' Dara laughed. 'You should join the Dramatic Society.'

'Maybe I will.' Orla tossed her head. 'At least my talents won't be wasted there.'

It was Muggins, again, who brought them the next piece of interesting information, as they were walking home from school one day.

'They've got a music school here,' he said excitedly, 'on Saturday mornings. Anyone can join.'

'Oh, yeah?' Mackey scoffed. 'I'll learn the violin, so, and do duets with Harold at the Feis!'

'No, they don't do things like that! They have classes for guitars and drums and keyboards and things .... That's how the school rock band started up.'

'Hey, I wouldn't mind learning the guitar,' Jonathan said.

'Nor me,' Felicity exclaimed.

'But we don't *have* guitars,' Orla pointed out. 'If I know my folks, they'll make me wait and get one for Christmas.'

'They've thought of that already,' Muggins told them triumphantly. 'Beginners' classes start after Christmas, too.'

Mackey's eyes had lit up. 'I'm going to ask my ma if I can learn the drums. I've always wanted to learn them properly.'

'She'll never let you!' Dara scoffed. 'Where would you practise? The neighbours would complain about the noise.'

Mackey looked smug. 'I'll practise at the pub, of course. My da has a soundproof room in the basement. He has gigs there, and he hires it out for practice sessions, too. One of the fellas in the pub is a deadly drummer — he's given me a few lessons already. He'll be able to get me a second-hand set of drums, no bother.'

The gang stared at Mackey in astonishment.

'Lucky beggar!' said Muggins enviously.

'How come you never told us about this before?' Orla demanded.

Mackey shrugged. 'You never asked.'

'Would your dad let us practise there if we got a group together?'

Mackey nodded. 'Course he would.'

'Hang on!' protested Joan. 'We haven't even started lessons yet.'

'But we will. Why not?' Orla was more excited than the gang had seen her in a long time. 'I fancy being a rock singer, too.' She did some pirouettes along the pavement, then turned to face them, holding a pretend microphone and dancing provocatively.

'Go-go girl!' Mackey shouted. 'But the clothes are all wrong — you need to strip a bit!'

If he thought he was going to make Orla blush, he was sadly disappointed. Orla stuck her tongue out at him. 'I will, too! Just you wait ... you'll be scarlet to your little eardrums, Ignatius McCarthy!'

☆   ☆   ☆

In the middle of a double German class one afternoon, Felicity was sent to give a message to the headmaster. She was glad to escape. Mrs Pratsche was in a foul humour, as none of the class seemed to be able to grasp basic German.

The corridors were quiet. Felicity could just hear the murmur of lessons from behind closed doors. As she was about to knock on the headmaster's office door, he came rushing out, clutching a mass of electrical cables.

Felicity gave him Mrs Pratsche's message. He nodded, then shoved the cables into her arms. 'Bring these up to the hall — and stay there and help if you're needed.'

'But ... but I've got German,' Felicity stuttered, surprised.

'I'll tell Mrs Pratsche. I'm going that way — I've got a meeting.' The headmaster hurried off with a distracted air.

Felicity stared at the pile of stuff she was holding, then made her way slowly down the corridor to the school hall. She pushed open the door with her elbow.

The hall was empty, chairs stacked neatly along the walls. Up on stage was Hunk. He was surrounded by amplifiers and lights and microphones, and he was busily trying to untangle a tight bunch of cables.

Felicity stood staring at him until, without looking up, he said, 'Well, come on in — or are you going to stand there all day?'

Felicity, blushing furiously, did as she was told. She approached the stage, and he signalled to her to come up by the stairs at one side. She climbed the stairs, clutching her load tightly against her chest.

Hunk glanced up at what she was carrying and said, 'That's one lot, anyway. Just drop them over there, will you?' He nodded towards the back of the stage.

Felicity put the cables down on the floor and stood, not sure what to do next.

'Well, aren't you going to give me a hand with these, then? Here!' Hunk threw her the end of a cable, and she had to move smartly to catch it before it fell. 'You hold tightly onto that, and don't let go,' he warned. 'Some eejit has been playing cat's cradle with our equipment.'

Hunk proceeded to try and unweave the tangled cables, concentrating on his task. Felicity watched him. He was OK-looking, but nothing to get too excited about. His hair was loose today, falling down in a curtain around his face as he bent over. He flicked it back with a toss of his head.

'Done at last! Would you believe it?' Hunk was holding three separate cables, and there was a grin on his face. He looked directly at Felicity for the first time.

His eyes were very blue and piercing. They seemed to bore right into her soul. Felicity felt a slow blush rise from her neck to her forehead. She could see now why Orla was smitten.

'What's your name?' Hunk asked. 'Mine's Paul, but everyone calls me Hunk.'

'I know,' Felicity stammered, mortified at her blushing. 'Mine's Felicity.'

'Nice name — happiness, joy. Well, Felicity, I think we've cracked it. Time to plug in.'

He took his red guitar from behind an amplifier. He was busy for a moment, plugging things in; then he slung the guitar strap over his shoulder and the red guitar was in place again, right across his middle. He strummed a few chords.

Felicity started to giggle.

Hunk stopped playing. 'What's so funny, then?'

'Nothing ... oh, nothing!' Felicity squirmed with embarrassment.

'You must have been amused at something. Come on, share the joke.' His eyes were boring into hers again, but kindly.

'It's just something stupid — something my friend calls you. We used to see you walking around with your guitar .... She calls you "Red Belly" ....'

Hunk was staring at her in astonishment.

Felicity, totally embarrassed now, blurted anxiously, 'It's not meant to be rude or anything. It's a name that means a lot to us — it comes from this brilliant tree we used to have ....'

Suddenly, she was telling him everything — about the gang, the woods, their fight to save the Red Belly, and the terrible storm that had finally finished it all.

Felicity knew she was babbling, but she couldn't help herself. She hadn't talked about the Red Belly for weeks — she hadn't really talked about it since it had fallen down. Her mother didn't encourage it; she wanted Felicity to get on with things. The rest of the gang didn't seem interested any more. But it was all there inside Felicity, screaming to get out.

She talked and talked, unable to stop. Hunk listened without once attempting to interrupt.

Finally it was all said. Felicity felt utterly drained and, suddenly, rather foolish.

There was a faraway look on Hunk's face.

'Red Belly,' he mused. 'Red Belly. What a name! We've never been happy with ours ....'

Felicity froze as she realised what he meant. 'Oh, no — please — you can't use that! I shouldn't have told you. Oh, me and my big mouth!'

Hunk turned to face her. 'We're going places, you know. We may be just a school rock group at the moment — but when our Leaving Cert. is over .... People are interested already, important people. We're heading for the big time. The only thing we're missing is the right name. Red Belly would be perfect!'

'You can't use it,' Felicity wailed. 'You can't. The others would know I told you. They'd never speak to me again. Please ... please don't!'

'What are their names — these others?'

Felicity, totally confused now, told him. He made her describe each member of the gang. When she came to Mackey, Hunk said, 'Ah, yes ... the one who's always smoking behind the bicycle sheds.'

Felicity fell silent. How had she got herself into this?

'Well, Felicity Red Belly, we'd very much like to have your name for our group. We'll be doing the big Hallowe'en disco here in school. It'd be nice to have the name up and running by then — get it painted on our gear and all. You'd enjoy seeing that, wouldn't you?'

'I wouldn't see it anyway,' Felicity said. 'I'm not

allowed to go to discos.'

Hunk laughed. 'You'll be going to this one. It's school policy to socialise as well as study. Your folks will be getting a note home about it. They'll have no choice. Now, what about this name? We won't use it without permission, so will you talk to your friends?'

'They won't agree,' Felicity protested desperately. 'And they'll kill me for telling you in the first place.'

Hunk was staring at her with his blue, blue eyes. He was quietly persistent. 'You'll ask them, anyway?'

Felicity nodded miserably.

☆   ☆   ☆

When she told the gang, their reaction was every bit as bad as she had expected.

'How could you?' Orla railed. 'Now he knows I was watching him. Ohhh ... I don't *believe* this!'

'You told him my name? He's a bloody *prefect*!' Mackey screeched. 'Thanks a heap, Felicity!'

'He'll think we're a right bunch of kids, playing with trees,' Jonathan raged. 'It'll be all over the school by morning.'

'No, it won't .... He's not like that ....' Felicity tried to explain.

'We'll be a laughing-stock,' Joan said angrily. 'You'd no business saying that about me.'

'Or me,' said Muggins. 'You told him my nickname!'

'I haven't even been up a stupid tree for over a year,' Dara complained. 'Why did you have to include me? Why did you have to tell about any of us, anyway?'

'He asked,' Felicity said.

'Blabbermouth!' Mackey snorted.

'I'm never speaking to you again!' Orla fumed. 'Joan's right. We'll be the laughing-stock of the school!'

☆   ☆   ☆

Things didn't get any better over the next few days. The gang ignored Felicity. Even at home, Jonathan refused to talk to her.

Felicity took to staying in the classroom for lunch, instead of going out into the schoolyard. Her efforts to re-establish relations with the gang were met by cold-shouldering. It was the most miserable time of her life.

Felicity's classmates noticed what was going on and tried to help by including her in their conversations. It was nice of them, but it didn't ease the pain of being rejected by her friends.

She tried to stay clear of Hunk. The seniors' class-rooms were in a separate part of the school, but Felicity had to keep a sharp eye out in the corridors, in case he was on prefect duty. Once or twice she spotted him in the distance and hid in the toilets until he was gone.

One day, after such a sighting, she emerged from the toilets, having checked the corridor carefully first. She'd only taken a few steps when she felt a hand on her shoulder.

Hunk! He must have been watching for her from a classroom.

'Hi, Felicity,' he said casually. 'You're a hard person to track down.'

'I'm in a hurry,' Felicity said furiously.

'Did you ask your friends?'

'Yes, I did, and thanks to you they're not speaking to me any more. I *told* you that would happen. But you're only interested in your stupid band!' Angrily she shrugged off Hunk's hand, which was still on her shoulder. 'Now leave me alone!'

She walked quickly up the corridor, hoping he wouldn't follow. Just as she turned the corner, she looked back. He was still standing in the same spot, staring after her.

☆   ☆   ☆

The next day, Felicity was handed a note asking her to
meet Hunk during lunch-hour. The note was quite
specific: Room 10 at one o'clock — not before. She
would have ignored the note, only it had been handed
to her by another prefect. She couldn't be sure that it
wasn't about school business.

She ate her lunch alone in her classroom. She was
really supposed to be outside, but she'd sneaked back
in when the yard prefect wasn't looking.

At one o'clock she made her way to Room 10. She
could hear voices inside. Slowly she opened the door ....

They were all there — Orla and Joan and Jonathan,
Dara, Muggins and Mackey. Hunk was sitting on a
desk, talking to them. Up at the top of the room were
three guys Felicity had never seen before.

She stood still, taken by surprise.

'Well, come in,' Hunk said. 'You *do* like standing in
doorways!'

Felicity came in and shut the door.

'Meet the rest of the band,' said Hunk, pointing to
the three strangers. 'Doxie, Eyeball and Plankton —
otherwise known as Hugh, Jody and Shane.' They
came across and shook hands with Felicity.

'Oh, Felicity! You won't believe it!' Orla burst out.
'We're going to have free admission to all their gigs,
starting right now. We'll be guests of honour!'

'And when they get rich and famous, they'll pay for
us to come and see them do a gig, anywhere in the
world we like!' Muggins was beside himself with
excitement. 'Even China, or Alaska.'

'Doxie's going to give me lessons on the drums,'
Mackey raved, 'tell me all the tricks.'

'They're going to help us with our guitars, too!'
Jonathan was elated.

'When we get them,' added Joan.

Dara was staring at Hunk in open admiration.

'That's pretty well it!' Hunk laughed. 'Story told, before I could get a word in edgeways.'

Felicity sat down. It was all too much to take in.

'You've agreed, then?' she asked the gang.

'Course we have!' Mackey exclaimed. 'We'd be bonkers not to.'

'You should have explained properly,' Orla chided her. 'We didn't know it was a deal like this.'

'I didn't know either,' Felicity said, looking at Hunk.

He smiled at her and gave her a conspiratorial wink. 'All settled, so?'

Felicity nodded.

'That's it, then. Will you take my word on the deal, or do you want it on paper?'

Joan answered quickly, 'On paper, please. It's a contract.'

'Right,' said Hunk. 'We'll draw up something tonight and you can sign it tomorrow — OK?'

They all agreed.

'Good old Red Belly,' Mackey said softly. 'Down and out, but still coming up trumps!'

There was an atmosphere of high excitement in Conker Hill Secondary as Hallowe'en approached. Posters for the Red Belly gig and the disco were up all over the school. For their logo, the band had used a splash of red paint, uncannily like the one that had been on the tree. 'Red Belly' was scrawled across this in spiky writing. Everybody was remarking on the new name, but the gang kept quiet about their part in it. The band were practising every single day, after school, as the big night drew near.

Then — at last — it was Hallowe'en.

The gang met in the Kellys' house at half past six. They were going to call for Dara on the way to the gig. But first, they had to make sure they were properly turned out.

'Where's Mackey?' Jonathan asked. 'He's late.'

'He'll be along in a few minutes,' Orla said, looking mysterious.

Muggins went into Jonathan's bedroom, while Orla and Joan went into Felicity's room to put the finishing touches to themselves.

Orla had surpassed herself. She was wearing green nail polish, green and purple eyeshadow, and a black skirt so short and tight that Felicity said in awe, 'How did your mum let you buy that?'

'She didn't,' Orla said airily. 'I borrowed it from a girl in school — might buy it from her.' She ran a hand over her cropped hair, which seemed to have grown little in the past two months, then took two large purple paper-clips out of her bag and proceeded to thread them carefully through the holes in her earlobes.

Felicity and Joan stared, open-mouthed. Feat accomplished, Orla examined her reflection with satisfaction.

'There,' she said. 'All done.'

'I look boring,' Joan wailed.

'Use your hair gel, like you were going to,' said Orla, 'and here — I've brought loads of stuff with me.' She emptied a bag of lipsticks and eyeshadows onto the bed. 'Help yourselves,' she invited them.

Felicity glanced at her own reflection. She didn't look bad, she thought, even without make-up. Bwalya King, who sat beside her in class, had done her hair. Bwalya had long, black, frizzy hair, and she often wore it in a fall of tiny plaits. The plaits had fascinated Felicity ever since the beginning of term. When they had been talking about the Hallowe'en disco one day, and Felicity had complained about her own mousy hair, Bwalya had offered to plait hers too.

Felicity had gone to Bwalya's house the previous night. It had taken hours, but the result was worth every minute. Coloured threads and little beads had been woven into some of the plaits. Felicity hardly recognised herself with the curtain of tiny plaits falling to her shoulders, swinging every time she moved.

Joan was plastering wet-look gel onto her hair. She experimented a bit with different styles, but in the end she just smoothed it back sleekly. Then, satisfied so far, she put some of Orla's green eyeshadow on her eyelids.

Jonathan put his head through the doorway at one stage, to shouts of 'Get out!' from the girls. But he had time to spot Joan's jar of hair gel, which he bagged for Muggins and himself.

When the boys were finally allowed to join the girls, they looked most unlike their usual selves. Jonathan had a new black shirt, of which he was immensely proud. With his blond hair slicked back, he looked really cool. Muggins, using the gel, had twisted his hair into spikes that stuck out all over his head. It was suitably weird, to go with the T-shirt that Mackey had loaned him, which had very strange graphics all over it. Mackey had got it from the fella in the pub who had a rock band.

There was a commotion downstairs as Mackey arrived at last. He had on an old tracksuit, and his hair fell untidily around his face.

'You haven't taken much trouble with yourself,' said Joan.

Mackey just grinned.

'I'm doing Mackey,' Orla announced. 'Can we use your bedroom, Jonathan?'

Jonathan nodded.

'And nobody's to come in until we say so, OK?'

The others agreed, laughing.

'You'd better hurry up,' Muggins said. 'It's nearly time to meet Dara.' Now that he was ready, he was anxious to be off.

'Ten minutes,' Orla promised. 'That's all. Oh, Felicity — have you got an ice-cube?'

'An ice-cube!' Felicity spluttered. 'What do you want that for?'

But Orla wasn't giving anything away. Felicity fetched the ice-cube, and Orla took Mackey and her bag of tricks into Jonathan's room and firmly closed the door.

After ten minutes, there was still no sign of them. Jonathan went out onto the landing and banged on his bedroom door.

'Ten minutes are up! Are you finished?'

'Nearly ready — just five minutes more,' Orla called.

They waited another three minutes; then they all headed for Jonathan's room.

'Can we come in yet?' Felicity shouted.

'Just one sec!' Orla yelled. 'We're coming out.'

The bedroom door was flung open.

'Ta-da!' Orla sang, bowing and sweeping her arms dramatically towards Mackey.

The rest of the gang gasped, hardly recognising the apparition before them.

Mackey's head had been shaved. He was completely bald — and stuck through the top of one of his ears was a huge safety pin.

'Your mother will *kill* you!' Joan gasped.

'I know,' Mackey grinned. 'But it'll be worth it.'

He had discarded the shabby tracksuit and was wearing a pair of camouflage combat trousers from Army Bargains. The legs, being too long for him, were carefully rolled up. A khaki T-shirt and boots completed the look. The T-shirt had 'Peace' emblazoned across the front.

Muggins was gaping at Mackey's shaven head in amazement. 'How did you do that?' he demanded.

Orla held up a pair of electric clippers. 'I was going to give him a Number Two, but then he decided to have the lot off.'

'Where did you get that clipper thing?'

'Bought it ages ago, with money from my savings account.'

'And Mum's been wondering why your hair hasn't grown!'

Orla laughed.

Joan was examining the safety pin in Mackey's ear. 'Are you trying to give him blood poisoning?'

'I sterilised it,' Orla said calmly. 'I boiled it for ages before I came here, and just to be sure, I sterilised it again in the flame from a match.' She pointed back into the bedroom. On the table in front of the window were a box of matches, a cork, and an almost-melted ice-cube.

'The ice-cube deadens the pain,' she explained.

'I don't mind pain,' Mackey said. But he was grinning, enormously pleased with himself.

Orla gathered up the sheet of newspaper on the floor, which contained all Mackey's hair, and shoved it into the wastepaper basket.

'Ready!' she declared. 'Let's go and call for Dara. He'll be wondering where we are.'

☆   ☆   ☆

As they walked to the village, the streets were full of strange creatures. They could hear shouts of 'Trick or treat!' and 'Help the Hallowe'en party!' as groups of masked children accosted neighbours on their door-steps.

'This is the first time we haven't dressed up for Hallowe'en,' said Felicity wistfully.

'What do you call that?' laughed Jonathan, pointing at Orla.

'Well, you know what I mean. It's the first year we haven't gone around knocking on doors.'

'That's for children,' said Joan haughtily.

'Still and all ... if we didn't have this disco I think I might have gone around again.'

'Me too,' said Muggins. 'Maybe we could bang on a few doors on our way?' He looked at the others hopefully.

Orla shook her head. 'You can't have it both ways, Muggins. Nobody would give us anything dressed like this. They'd say we look too old.'

'But we're not!' Muggins protested. 'Not really.'

'We're in-betweens,' Joan said. 'Neither one thing nor the other.'

'We don't need labels,' said Felicity firmly. 'We're ourselves, and that's enough.'

☆   ☆   ☆

There was a huge crowd in the school hall. Most of them were packed close to the stage. The gang had to be content with a place halfway down the hall. People were crowding in behind them. Everyone was in a high good humour.

'How are we going to have room to dance?' Jonathan asked, looking around.

'There'll be tons of room when everyone spreads out,' Orla said breezily. 'They just want to listen to the band first.'

The blue velvet stage curtains were firmly closed. The crowd waited, talking excitedly.

Dara, who hadn't taken a great deal of trouble with his appearance, had been giving the others strange sidelong glances ever since they'd collected him.

'You should have told me you were getting all dressed up,' he said, annoyed.

'We're not all dressed up. We're just a bit different,' Mackey smirked.

'Hey, Mackey!' Felicity called wickedly. 'That girl you sit beside hasn't taken her eyes off you since you came in!'

'I know,' Mackey growled. 'I'll give her a black eye if she doesn't stop gawking!' But he didn't look exactly displeased.

The lights dimmed, and there was a big 'Ooooh!' from the crowd.

With a roll of drums, the stage curtains were slowly drawn apart.

The first thing the gang noticed was the Red Belly logo on the drums. Then they saw the T-shirts that the band were wearing. These were black, with the big splash of red in front; right across it ran the name 'Red Belly', in spiky white letters. They looked fantastic.

Doxie was playing the drums. Eyeball was gyrating in front of the keyboard. Plankton and Hunk had their guitars at the ready.

A huge roar went up from the audience, and people started screaming.

Hunk stepped forward with a microphone, putting up a hand for silence. The crowd gradually hushed, until all was quiet. Hunk started to speak, his voice eerily everywhere as it came from amplifiers set up all around the hall.

'Hi, everybody, and welcome to the very first gig by Red Belly, the band of the future! As you all know, we've been on the go for a long time under another name. But tonight is a fresh beginning. We owe our fantastic new name to seven first-years, and I'd like you to give them a big round of applause — Felicity, Mackey, Orla, Joan, Jonathan, Muggins and Dara!'

The crowd clapped and clapped, half of them looking around in bewilderment, trying to see who they were meant to be clapping for. The gang squirmed with embarrassment. But Hunk didn't labour the point; within seconds, the attention was off them and back on the stage.

The crowd quietened as Hunk began to speak again.

'This is an important year for Red Belly. We have our Leaving Cert. to get out of the way first, but after that, things will happen pretty fast. I can tell you now that a record company is interested in us, and next summer we go on tour to Germany. There's a bright future ahead. Red Belly are poised to take the world by storm! But remember — when we're up there in the charts, when our name is blazing out from every newsstand, when our music is on everybody's lips — remember that it started right here ... tonight ... in this hall ... and you are all part of that.'

A resounding cheer went up from the crowd, echoing around the hall. Hunk held up his hand for silence again.

'So, to celebrate our new beginning, we've composed a special signature tune, and I'd like you all to join in at the end of each verse. I'll give you the signal.'

Hunk stepped back into his place, returning the microphone to its stand. He nodded to the rest of the band, and they swung straight into the first verse.

'Red Belly, Red Belly
Reach for the sky
Red Belly, Red Belly
High, high, high
Shout it, shout it
Wild and free
Red Belly, Red Belly
Who are we?'

'*Red Belly*!' roared the crowd, at a signal from Hunk.

Felicity's eyes filled with tears, and a hard, stinging lump constricted her throat. The band had launched enthusiastically into the second verse, but Felicity was no longer listening. Her thoughts were back with their own precious Red Belly, and, for a moment, the sense of loss was unbearable.

Then, strangely, she began to think of all the things in their attic at home: the discarded dolls, the building blocks, the games, the long-outgrown toys, once so dearly loved. With a sudden insight she realised that the Red Belly and all their happy times weren't gone — would never be truly gone. They were merely stored away in the attics of their hearts, to be retrieved and remembered whenever the need arose. A deep sense of peace stole through her with this thought, a sense of coming to terms with things. She was ready to face the future.

Felicity came out of her reverie. She glanced around at the rest of the gang, and knew by their faces that they were feeling much the same way.

Mackey caught her eye and, leaning forward, shouted, 'Maybe we should've kept the name for ourselves — made our own rock group.'

Felicity shook her head. 'No!' she shouted back. 'It was time to let go.'

'Go! Go! Go!' bawled the band, coming to the end of the second verse.

'Go! Go! Go!' roared the crowd, ecstatic.

Mackey grinned and linked his arm through Felicity's. They linked arms with the others then — Muggins and Joan on one side; Jonathan, Orla and Dara on the other. Together they swayed back and forward to the music, as the band swung into its final refrain ....

'Red Belly, Red Belly
We're going far
Red Belly, Red Belly
Reach for a star
Blazing through the heavens
With a bright red flame
For written on that star
Is a very special name ....'

'*Red Belly*!' screamed the gang, their voices joining hundreds of others in the hall, surging and swelling into one crazy, rapturous roar.

'*Red Belly*!'

The great sound soared to the ceiling and out the high open windows, floating away across the village and beyond, to where Conker Woods lay sleeping under the ever-changing sky.

RED BELLY

RED BELLY, RED BELLY
REACH FOR THE SKY
RED BELLY, RED BELLY
HIGH, HIGH, HIGH
SHOUT IT, SHOUT IT
WILD AND FREE
RED BELLY, RED BELLY
WHO ARE WE?

RED BELLY!

DREAMING TIME
HAS BEEN AND GONE
THIS IS THE ROAD
WE'RE TRAVELLING ON
THE WORLD SPINS FAST
THE WORLD SPINS SLOW
CATCH IT BY THE TAIL
AND GO! GO! GO!

RED BELLY, RED BELLY
WE'RE GOING FAR
RED BELLY, RED BELLY
REACH FOR A STAR
BLAZING THROUGH THE HEAVENS
WITH A BRIGHT RED FLAME
FOR WRITTEN ON THAT STAR
IS A VERY SPECIAL NAME ....

RED BELLY!

BY THE SAME AUTHOR

DON'T MISS ....

Up the Red Belly

'Joan always maintained that the trouble they got into that
summer was entirely due to the arrival of Mackey ....'

The Red Belly gang — Felicity, Jonathan, Mackey, Muggins,
Joan, Dara and Orla — are spending their summer holidays
in the woods and up their wonderful tree, the Red Belly.
Join them as they tangle with a ghost, get sussed
nicking gooseberries, stage a disastrous production of
Blood and Guts on Treasure Island — and much, much more!

ISBN 0-86327-530-3

Red Belly, Yellow Belly

For the Red Belly gang, the trouble really started when
Harold decided to set up a rival gang and call their tree the
Yellow Belly. They had to sort that little pest out — but
Harold takes his revenge in some very unexpected ways ....

And that's not all! What's lying in wait at the haunted gate-
house? Will Mackey and Dara ever learn to get on?
And why, oh why, are Felicity's parents making the gang
spend their summer tidying up horrible old Fitzy's garden?

ISBN 0-86327-640-7

Available from:
WOLFHOUND PRESS
68 Mountjoy Square, Dublin 1